THE LAST SHOT

by

AMY MATAYO

THE LAST SHOT

For Connie, Christy, Nicole, and Tammy

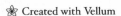 Created with Vellum

THE LAST SHOT

By

Amy Matayo

CHAPTER ONE

Teddy

I toss my phone on the table and take two steps away when another text comes through. She's persistent, I'll give her that. She's also out of her mind, something I've had to contend with for the last ten minutes, not to mention my entire life. Texting Dillon is the last thing I need to be doing right now, but ignoring her isn't in my DNA. I roll my eyes and pick up the phone again. She might be a thorn in my side, but she's been my best friend since birth. So even though the room is vibrating and I'm going to be late due to dreaming up ways to murder her, I don't want to hurt her feelings. Still...

"No, I won't be your maid of honor. Ask Sabrina."
Sabrina is our cousin. A girl makes more sense than me.

"I don't want Sabrina. I want you."
Her lightning-fast fingers are likely shooting sparks.
I text back.

"Will there be photographers?"
I can practically hear her sigh from here. It was a stupid question.

"Of course, there will be photographers. It's my wedding day. People tend to document those things. Come on, Teddy. Do it for me."

The sound of the guitar solo lead-in is what makes me cave. I'm expected onstage in less than sixty seconds. Fifty-two, to be exact. I've got the routine down to a science. Under normal circumstances, I would have enough time for a quick bathroom stop and a long swig of beer. As it stands, I'm debating Dillon's wedding details and my involvement in them. I have thirty-seven seconds left. Why am I being dragged into this now? Oh, that's right, because she's my cousin. And while she's proud of me, my career comes second to her wedding. Fair enough.

"Fine. But I'm not wearing a dress."

I'm going to regret this. I can already feel it.

"THANK YOU! We'll discuss details later. Knock 'em dead tonight."

I smile to myself, noticing she didn't agree to the no-dress thing. Dillon is her own person and rarely agrees to anything without a lengthy discussion. Still, I'm winning this debate. I may have just agreed to be her maid of honor under duress —*what the heck is wrong with me?*—but I won't be wearing pink taffeta to the party. I made that mistake when we were nine and Dillon talked me into a makeover complete with purple nail polish, sparkly pink eyeshadow, and her mother's Easter dress. My mother still has that lovely photo taped to her refrigerator at home and will not take it down, no matter how much I beg.

All around me, people do what I ask. Everyone except the ones who know me best. They tell me what I can do with my pseudo-demands, which usually involves me shoving large things up areas that would make sitting down impossible. It's what I love about them most.

"I will. I'll text you after it's over."

I hear my phone chime after I set it on the table, but the time for talking is over. Ten seconds. That's all I have. I jog three steps over and tuck myself onto the lift that will carry me up to the stage as adrenaline rushes through my bloodstream. No matter how many times I do this, it never gets old. Maybe it will one day, but today is not that day.

"Ready?" Josh, the stage coordinator, says as he reaches for the button that activates the lift.

My phone chimes again, but I nod, too filled with purpose to think about anything but what I'm doing. This career is what I've worked toward since the first day I picked up a guitar on my fifth birthday. To see it come to fruition is like holding the one thing you've always wanted in the palm of your hand and staring at it, so grateful for its presence that you're unable to look away. The people in the crowd are here for me, and I don't take a single second of that for granted. Tour life is exhausting when you've been on the road four months straight, but it's worth it.

The lift moves, and I'm on stage in three seconds. Camera flashes go off across the arena. Screams crescendo into mass hysteria. Spotlights blind me to anything but the front row. Like always, the whole display makes me smile.

Time to give Seattle a show they'll never forget.

———

What do maids of honor even do?

Nearing the end of the first song, I shake my head and climb onto the crane. The crane acts like a helicopter designed to fly me over the audience, allowing me to get up close and personal with those in the cheap seats. We use it now and later in the show, and both times are my favorite parts of the night. I remember seeing Tim McGraw when I was younger, simultaneously happy to be at the concert and sad to be stuck in the third section. We were so high that Tim appeared the size of an ant, and my head was woozy from the altitude. To be one of the lucky few on the floor, so close they could reach out and touch him, was a dream of mine that felt as impossible as flying to the moon.

This gives everyone an equal shot at reaching the stars, so to speak. At least for a few minutes.

The crane jerks to a start as it takes off, slowly raising me higher until I'm halfway across the stadium. I'm singing the second song, smiling at the crowd's frenzied reaction to my rapid approach. I love seeing the faces of those in the back even more than the faces of those on the front row, and tonight is no exception. Still, my thoughts won't slow down.

Seriously, will I be expected to throw Dillon a bachelorette party? Because I am not sitting through anything that involves male strippers. I don't care how much she expects me to.

Sometimes the strangest thoughts pop into my brain at the weirdest times. One hundred feet in the air, and all I can visualize are oiled men in black G-strings. I shudder at the mental image and sing the next line.

Last night in St. Louis, I couldn't shake a desire for tacos. The night before in Indianapolis, it was an unauthorized charge on my credit card bill I hadn't been able to solve, despite waiting on hold with a Visa representative for twenty minutes. And tonight, I'm currently three verses into our second song, and I can't stop envisioning myself in a dress. Photos splashed all over some cheap tabloid as both sides of the aisle take shots at my sexuality. I'm straight as a laser beam, but I've been down that road before, beginning with that stupid photo my mom still has hanging in her kitchen. *Keep my son out of a dress*, my father shouted when he saw it the first time. In response, my mother yelled *I will not,* and Super Glued the picture front and center to the door, hence its current placement. I learned a couple valuable lessons that day:

No one messed with my mother, and the choices you make when you're young may, in fact, haunt you forever.

Kind of like Dillon is haunting me now. I work to shove her out of my mind as I sing the last line.

"How's it going, Seattle?" I yell over the final notes. "We're so glad to be here!"

The crowd roars as they always do when they hear their hometowns mentioned. Seattle has a great music scene, but I'm always surprised by how much they love country. If a battle ensued between the north and south over who loves the genre more, it might just be a tie. We'll test that theory two weeks from tonight. That's when we're headlining at Madison Square Garden for the very first time.

When that show sold out in twenty minutes, a lifelong dream had been realized. To say I'm excited is a major understatement. It's been a while since I've been truly nervous; the thought of playing the Garden is more akin to terrifying. I grin behind me at Jack, my bassist, and laugh at the expression he makes on the overhead screen. It appears he's having an even better time tonight than me, and I'm the one flying through the air. I adjust my guitar strap and strum the opening note of the next song as flares shoot up on both sides of the stage. A frame of fireworks, just as we planned.

"This one's called *Up in Smoke!* I hope you guys enjoy it!" I lock eyes with a raven-haired beauty below me and wink. She screams at her friend beside her, both enjoying the hell out of this. More sparks spray on both sides of the stage, my cue to sing the first line.

"You say your name like a whisper, then bite your lip on a sigh..."

A boom goes off behind me, and the crane shakes. I frown when the lift stalls. This isn't supposed to happen. Only two sets of fireworks are scheduled to go off, and then I'm lifted higher for the third song. Stopping has never been part of the routine. I glance up at Jack on the JumboTron, but he's busy searching for the source of the noise, looking as confused as me. Maybe something fell. Maybe the sound was a reverberation. It doesn't happen often, and every arena is different, but sometimes, the acoustics are weaker in spots. This must be one of those times. Jack keeps playing, so I shrug off any hesitation and continue to sing.

I think about taking you home with me, wonder if you'd stay with me all night..."

Another boom, this one accompanied by screams that rise a little higher than the others. Screams still framed with excitement, but somehow also centered by terror. I'm not sure what I hear because I've never heard it before. Weirder still, the crane begins to lower at a rapid pace. I hold on with one hand and take another look at Jack, sending him a mental plea for clarity. *What's happening?* His eyes dart side-to-side, and he takes a step back. The show must go on, a mantra every entertainer lives by. I keep singing and glance at the rest of the band, thankful the lyrics come as naturally as my next breath. Rande is still drumming, but his arms have gone rigid in hesitation like they know the beat, but he's unsure whether to continue playing them. Tessa, Malik, and Christy keep singing back-up, but their arms hang limp, choreography all but forgotten. All eyes swing to me, the one in charge. Decision-making might come easier if I wasn't hovering over a crowd entirely alone. I look and feel like an idiot.

I turn back toward the audience and smile, more to reassure myself than them. So many are still dancing, still happy, that I keep going. Paranoia isn't anyone's best friend.

"It doesn't take much convincing, we park under the street lamp out front..."

Another boom, this one accompanied by a red flash to my right and an earsplitting crack. Paranoia, my ass. I'm out.

Heart hammering, pulse tripping, throat clogged with so much gunk I can barely get an airway, I stop singing and fall to one knee, hoping the bars enclosing me might offer some protection from whatever is happening around me.

I lock eyes with the raven-haired girl in front of me until she looks at her chest. Her fingers flutter upward as something that looks like blood—*why would it be blood?*—fans across her white shirt. The colors swirl together in a juxtaposition of irony, like seeing a crescent moon in broad daylight. She looks up to find me watching. Her eyes ask a hundred questions right before she crumples to the ground.

People scream.

Others run.

One door opens, and a few file out.

Two others remain locked, people banging on them and each other in a ring of frenzy.

As for me, I'm still suspended twenty feet in the air on one knee and terrified for my life. I rattle the cage to no avail.

Another boom. Dozens fall to the ground in stunned shock.

"Get me down!" I yell and rattle the cage again, not recognizing the sound of my own voice. I've never shrieked so wildly or sounded so terrified. The crane lowers so quickly that I have to hang on with both hands to avoid tumbling out. While I'm still four feet in the air, someone grabs me from behind and yells my name, but I'm too absorbed in the sight of mass chaos to turn around.

Before we reach the ground, I'm pulled over the side of the cage in one swift motion; my back scrapes against metal, my jeans rip on the thigh. I'm not bleeding, but my skin throbs in both spots from the roughness of the movement. A female voice yells a string of words I can't make out—names, dates, cries for help, I think—but I'm too numb and on edge to know for sure. I'm confused and entirely certain. Excitable and sick. My vision blurs like I'm living out someone else's life, like I'm here but not. I'm both inside my body, and outside watching like a spectator.

I think someone in this arena is shooting at us.

I know someone is dragging me backward.

I'm incapable of comprehending any of it.

Movement catches my eye, a blur of black here and gone before I can focus. My heart beats behind my eyes. Adrenaline pumps into my throat. Nothing in my body feels right or familiar. These things happen in other states and other towns. In churches and shopping malls, at gas stations and schools. They cover it on the news; it's heartbreaking and frustrating, but it always happens to someone else.

It never happens to you.

People move like nervous mice, going everywhere and nowhere. They hide under chairs, kick at doors, step on each other, rush the aisles, look for an escape. A door opens. A flash of red goes off to my right; another gunshot, this one close to my ear. I duck and holler and half-crawl a few feet, survival instinct clawing upward to choke out every other emotion. A century passes in ten seconds. A hand grips my forearm tighter. A voice shouts in my ear.

"Move! Faster! Now!"

I trip over a shoe in the aisle, but the hand doesn't let go. The shoe looks like a child's, but there's no time to take a second glance. Blood. All I see is blood. A sunburst. An emptying of life. Red on black on white, a foreign flag inside a Seattle arena.

Why is a child's shoe just lying on the floor?

A door opens, and I'm flung inside a room the size of a closet. My back slams against the far wall and I fall to the floor.

I think I hit my head.

Or maybe my head hit me.

I stare and stare and stare and stare.

I rock back and forth and back and forth.

My heart swells in my chest and explodes like a hand grenade. Shrapnel goes everywhere and cuts everything in its path. My limbs, my brain, my throat, my lungs. I can't breathe. I can't think. I can't move. I can't see.

I rock and rock and rock and rock.

It's pitch black in this room, but the nightmare is vivid.

People are dying out there, and it's all my fault.

———

Jane

I've practiced this so many times.

Follow protocol.

Stick to the routine.

Check the doors, secure the premises, protect the target, hand on your gun, don't shoot unless the shot is clear.

I've heard about it, watched it, sympathized, mourned.

We all have, every single American, each one of us.

You analyze it, scrutinize it, proselytize it because you have all the answers: *"this is what should happen, this is how things should be handled, this is what we should learn."* You think you know what you'll do. You believe you'll fight, grab a weapon and take the shooter down, enlist the help of others and form a mob mentality, essentially save the day and win a medal of honor for your immense bravery under intense pressure. Never in your wildest dreams do you think you'll just sit on the floor of a closet, too paralyzed with fear and confusion to move.

Blood rushes between my ears. I rock back and forth, aware I'm mimicking the movement of another. Apparently, terror sings the same song for all of us.

Stick to the job, stick to the job, stick to the job.

I blink in the darkness and feel my body go still, determination taking over as anger moves up and outward. This will not beat me. I will win this fight.

I'm suddenly aware of Teddy Hayes sitting beside me.

I open my mouth to reassure him when someone screams outside the door.

Teddy lunges forward.

I leap to catch him and connect with his calf.

What the heck is he doing?

CHAPTER TWO

Teddy

A woman screams. Feet rush by the door. I need to help. I can't just leave them out there to die.

I lurch forward and reach for the handle to pull a few other people in here with me, but a hand slaps me away. I'm trapped in here with a stranger whose face I haven't seen and whose intentions aren't known. Maybe this is the killer. Maybe I was shoved in here to die. I reach for the handle again and get the same reaction.

"Stop slapping me," I shout. All the benefits of celebrity can't help me now.

"Stop trying to open the door, and I will." A female voice threat-whispers in my ear.

"I don't hide in closets."

"You do now. If you want to stay alive, then be quiet." She's breathing heavily, same as me.

"Who are you? What is happening out there?" I whisper back, deciding maybe she's right and silence is the best route. Still, until I have answers, I don't take orders from anyone.

"I'm a security guard the arena hired to keep you safe. So

starting now, I'm your personal bodyguard. Someone out there has a gun. If you want them to start shooting at us, by all means, keep arguing with me and open the door."

The fight drains out of me.

My bodyguard? None of this makes sense. We did everything right.

"How the hell is someone shooting?" I ask. There are bag checks set up at every entrance to prevent this sort of thing. Full-body scans and random pat-downs. Even *I* have to go through them.

How did this get past anyone?

"How...?"

My head spins with a thousand questions, but I stop talking. My hands fist my hair and pull, the pain somehow grounding me to the here and now. I lean forward with my head in my hands, my back against the door. The walls are closing in. I'm trapped in here, and she's telling me I can't leave. For how long? It's dark and cold and I think I'm starting to choke. I can't breathe. It's too small. It's too dark. It's too familiar. The walls are closing in until wood and paint and drywall are the only things I feel and smell and see. Claustophobia doesn't have an expiration date, and mine is going on fifteen years.

Everything is falling apart on the other side of the door.

I'm falling apart in here.

———

Jane

My heart hurts from all the pounding.

My stomach is seasick from all the rolling.

My throat burns from all the not breathing.

I reach for my walkie to call someone, my chest caving in on itself when I hear it rattle like a screw has come loose from the inside. I growl low and harsh. Can bad things please stop happening? I push the button and press the device to my mouth and test it, knowing what I'll find. Teddy Hayes is terrified, and it's my job to calm him down. How am I supposed to do that if I can't call for help? If I can't calm myself down either? I swallow and attempt both anyway.

"Andy, can you hear me? Eric, come in." Nothing but silence interrupted by faint bursts of static. I wait a beat and start again. "Andy, it's Jane. Please give me your location." More broken static greets me, not a single voice replies. My walkie must have broken when bodies smashed into me as I was reaching for Teddy. It fell to the floor as I hauled him over the side of that cage, but I managed to grab it before we ran under the stage.

We're under the catwalk on the opposite side of the stage, but I don't think Teddy realizes it. This room is meant for quick costume changes in between songs. I checked it an hour ago. There's a white cotton shirt identical to the one he's wearing now and a row of six water bottles pushed against the wall. That's it for supplies. No air vent or outside access, and the door is locked and will stay that way until it's safe enough to open. It could be minutes or hours from now, both of which already seem like an eternity.

The news is bad all by itself, but it's catastrophic considering my cell phone battery is already lit up yellow and currently has no service. I try to make a call, but there's a stadium filled with thousands of people, undoubtedly attempting to call for help. The screen spins but nothing happens. I turn the power down to the lowest level to save battery and keep my eyes on it, just in case the No Service status changes. After a couple minutes, the battery goes down another two percent, so I shut off the screen completely.

I've never felt as painfully inadequate as I feel in this moment, like a walk-on trying to make it in the big leagues. I have three years as a bodyguard already behind me, but none feel adequate against this. Concerts are my least favorite job, but every once in awhile, I'll take them for selfish reasons. Case in point, this one. I only applied for this gig to score a friend's new boyfriend free tickets to Teddy's concert, which now seems like a particularly pathetic way to boost their relationship. Now I'm mentally scrambling for a way out of this mess. One that won't have me headlining news stories as the person directly responsible for Teddy Hayes's death.

Good lord, what have I gotten myself into?

"Is there any chance you have a phone?" I ask Teddy, putting as much authority into my tone as one can when whispering.

"No, I've never needed one onstage." In the history of the English language, words have never had such a razor-sharp edge.

"Great. Mine has no service." I try another call just to prove my point.

His breath comes out long and shaky. It's interesting the way you hear things when sight has been stripped away. It's black as ink inside this room, but I can't afford to waste my phone's battery for something as trivial as being able to see. The light may also give away our whereabouts, something I can't risk.

"I always leave my phone in the dressing room. Right now, I'm regretting that decision."

I take a deep breath, one filled with stops and starts. It's hard to get any air when your lungs are squeezed in a vice. It's made more difficult when you're required to appear the brave one.

"It probably wouldn't work now anyway." Words meant to sound reassuring come out sounding defeated. Because they are. We're screwed. Stuck in a six by seven space with no immediate way out. I say a quick prayer heavenward that this disaster ends quickly. *What is going on out there? And who on earth is doing the shooting?*

We sit with our own thoughts, too focused on listening to do much else. Outside this door, people are screaming, people are running, things are smashing together. All we can do is sit and listen and pray that a few are making it to safety. *"You're here to protect the concert-goers and Teddy Hayes and his band. Should anything go wrong, the closest person to Teddy needs to get him to safety. Understood?"*

We'd all nodded in agreement, a silent pledge to do just that. The arena management hired me with that single expectation, and I won't let them down. Still, it's terrifying to feel powerless, especially with every blast of a gunshot. Every few seconds, another one sounds, and I feel Teddy jump. There's no way to know if this is the work of one person or more. The only thing I know for certain is that this attack was planned. The moment I made contact with Teddy Hayes, I glanced back at my partner, Andy, as he shoved his body against the closest exit—I presume to help people escape. That door didn't budge, not even an inch.

It was then that I knew: Some doors in this arena are locked. Maybe even barricaded shut. Not all, but definitely the ones closest to us. But it's common protocol to keep doors easily accessible, maybe even slightly ajar during an event as large as this one. Insurance companies require it, venues demand it, artists insist on it. Encasing fifteen thousand people into a space they can't easily leave is a nightmarish situation, not to mention a public relations nightmare most people couldn't recover from. If not personally, then most definitely financially. I was here two hours before this particular show started, and there's no doubt in my mind that this venue followed protocol. I checked several doors myself to make sure they could be easily opened. At the time, they did.

Someone broke through security and locked them.

"So, you're my bodyguard?" Teddy breaks the long silence, keeping his whisper low. "I've never seen you before. I can't even see you now, and I certainly didn't see you before you pulled me in here." He shifts, and there's something in his tone. It sounds a lot like distrust. I open my mouth to reassure him that he can trust me to keep him safe, but he keeps going. "Where is Bill or Steve or one of my normal guys? I mean, no offense but you're—"

He stops talking, and I roll my eyes in the dark. It isn't distrust, it is a lack of confidence in my skill.

"I'm a woman?" Suddenly I want him to say that to my face. Just because he's a rock star doesn't mean he can talk down to me.

"No." His voice is firm. "I was going to say 'you're a stranger.' But since you're the one bringing it up..."

I don't push it. I deserve to be put in my place for the assumption, but it's a line I've heard at least a hundred times before. It's a man's world, the one I'm working in. Personally, I've made peace with it. It's the jerks on the outside that drag my insecurities front and center without asking permission.

Except this time, I'm the jerk.

I sigh. "Look, obviously I'm a woman. And I'm on edge, so I'm sorry I made an assumption. I swear I'll do everything in my power to keep you safe," I whisper. And I mean it. If someone wants to kill him, they'll have to kill me first. He's silent for so long, it begins to worry me.

I can hear him biting a fingernail, and the mental image ushers in a softness I don't often feel. He may be one of the biggest stars in country music, but right now he's simply a guy who's afraid for his life. After all, signs most likely point to Teddy Hayes being the target. There are two options here, neither one more pleasant than the other: either someone wanted to shoot up the arena for the fame alone, or someone wanted to be famous for killing Teddy Hayes. Either way, Teddy is the common denominator. Everyone in the audience is collateral damage.

"What about you?" he whispers.

I frown. "What about me?"

"Who's going to keep you safe?"

His voice is so protective my heart snags inside my chest. In the three years I've been doing this job, no one has ever asked me that. Not even my mother, though I suppose that isn't much of a surprise.

"I suppose that will be up to me as well." I try a little laugh to mask the reality that I am currently falling a little bit apart, but it's emotionless. What does it say about me that the slightest hint of care has me going soft? I can't afford to be pathetic.

I straighten my back and press my ear against the door to listen. Things are quiet for the moment. I feel, rather than see, Teddy move closer to me. He must be listening as well, because his breath keeps feathering my cheek. Knowing we're only inches apart has me suddenly thankful for the darkness.

"I don't hear anything," he whispers. "Do you think it's over?"

No, I don't. It's the calm before the storm. I'm about to say as much when another gunshot cracks through the silence and says it all for me. Teddy leaps backward so fast that for a moment, I worry he's been hit.

"Are you alright?" I scramble on my hands and knees to find him, frantic to make contact with something, anything. I manage to locate his thigh and grip it a little too hard. At least I think it's his thigh. This is no time for timidity. I pat upward on his body, feeling anywhere and everywhere for a wound like I've been trained to do.

"I'm okay," he rasps, clutching my hand to still my movements. "Physically, anyway. Mentally, I'm a freaking mess."

I slump against the wall and fight tears without letting go of his hand. He's claimed it so fiercely inside his own, I'm not sure I could anyway. With my other hand, I reach for my phone to check for service. Try as I might, I still can't make the stupid thing work.

———

Only a few minutes later, a bloodcurdling cry sounds from outside the room, so close it's as if someone is being stabbed only inches from us. The fear in my chest shifts until it's lodged inside my throat. You train and train, practice responding to situations from one angle and another until you have your reactions locked tight and down to a science. But no one tells you that hypothetically being terrorized and actually being terrorized are not at all the same thing.

"What's happening out there?" Teddy whisper-cries directly into my ear as if he's afraid the sound might escape through the cracks if he attempts to speak any other way. He sniffs, and my grip on his hand tightens.

"I don't know. Just please be completely still." He doesn't move or speak again. Neither one of us does. As determined as I am to protect him, I'm equally as determined to live. We're both sitting with backs against the wall, breathing heavily and not breathing at all, terror making it hard for our lungs to fully function. He tightens his hold on my hand, and I'm oddly grateful. Until I have a handle on the situation...until I can grasp some meaning behind what is happening, I need something to hold onto. Something to keep my own sanity intact. Something to keep me strong instead of melting into a fear-laden puddle like I want to. Personal space doesn't exist here.

"Did you see the shooter?" he asks. "Any idea if they're acting alone?"

"They almost always act alone, but no, I didn't see the shooter. I did see my partner trying to open an exit door close by. It wouldn't budge. I personally checked that door before the concert, and it opened just fine."

I feel his eyes on me, imploring and unbelieving. "You mean everyone's locked in the arena with no way out?"

"Not everyone. There's no way one person could contain this many people. But the doors closest to us were locked. A lot of people are trapped, and I still haven't heard a siren or any outside noises at all."

It isn't an uncommon scenario, but I can feel the weight of his shock as it settles into his mind. Hundreds, possibly thousands of people trapped in this arena while a ruthless, attention-seeking asshole picks them off one by one, all of them here because Teddy Hayes sold them a ticket. If guilt had a shape, it would have two arms and legs and a head undoubtedly hanging in undeserved shame. Teddy didn't do this, but I doubt anyone could convince him otherwise.

"I haven't heard anything either," he whispers. "Except for screams."

Another gunshot ricochets through the air as if the shooter is mocking Teddy himself. Maybe he is.

Madmen don't respect anything. Not money or power or even life itself. Certainly nothing as trivial as fame.

Fame means nothing if you don't make it out alive.

———

A man's wild, psychotic demands cut through the air on the other side of the door.

"Everybody down! Everybody down now!" The words are followed by a mass of shrieks and cries, and the energy inside this room shifts from twenty watts to a hundred in the span of a single heartbeat. A bullet pummels through the door and whizzes over our heads, and I clamp my hand over my mouth to trap all the sounds threatening to escape. He is here, and we are dead. No, we are alive. We are alive, but I can't breathe. He is here, and he will find us, and he will kill us.

I barely remember my training.

Do your job.

Do your job.

The mantra doesn't help one bit. This stiff shirt is choking me, so I unbutton the first two buttons and pull at the collar. That doesn't help because it's my throat. My throat is choking me, and I have no way to make it stop. Pulling at one's throat only causes more problems, and I have enough to deal with right now.

I squeeze my hand into a fist, then press my forehead to the ground and remind myself to breathe. When did breathing become something one forgets? In. Out. Eyes closed. Eyes open. I've recited a different mantra in my head three times through before I realize what I'm saying.

I am in charge, I know what to do.

I am in charge, I know what to do.

I am in charge, I know what to do.

I say it a few more times to get it in my brain, then stop when I think it's taken hold. This isn't the time to panic. I may not have faced an actual mass shooting before, but I have trained extensively for one. I would bet money that Teddy hasn't, which means I need to get myself together now. I am in charge, and I know what to do.

"What should we do?" he whispers.

"We should stay very still and quiet until he walks away." I let go of his hand and slide onto my stomach to peer under the door, careful not to kick anything or make a sound that might alert anyone to our whereabouts. The man is still screaming *everyone down!* like no one is actually listening, but I have no doubt they're obeying. A pair of sneakers are right outside the door, directly in front of my vision, white leather and new as though bought and saved for this special occasion. I blink at them, alternately baffled by the man's choice of jogging shoes and willing those same shoes to move away. Combat boots would have made more sense. The mind thinks weird things when under intense pressure.

"Well?" Teddy says.

"He's still here. Don't talk." My words are a hoarse whisper. I can barely hear over the frightening sound of cries and my own pounding heartbeat. Guilt that I want the shooter to move away from us and toward the crowd eats at my conscience, even if this is my job. Fear twists my lungs into nothing but useless organs screaming for an inhale. Slowly, I try. Teddy inches closer to me, so close I can feel his chest and then his thighs as he settles into place. His breath lands on my right shoulder. It's frightening to be inside this dark closest. I'm not even attempting to wear a brave face; no one can see it anyway.

"Should you try your phone again?" he asks. "Maybe you'll have service now."

I won't, but I reach behind me to slide the phone out of my pocket and hand it to him, glancing over at the faint glow of light that illuminates his mouth when he turns it on. He punches a couple numbers, then holds the phone between his fingers. His hands are the only thing I can see, but they're saying a lot in the way they've gone limp and still.

"Still nothing," he says.

"I know. I tried it a couple minutes ago."

"I guess there just hasn't been enough time for the police to organize a rescue," he says.

It feels like hours, but it's only been three minutes max. There hasn't been enough time for the world to know that hell has descended on a concert arena in Seattle, locking several thousand innocent souls inside its fiery grip and refusing to let go. There hasn't been enough time for news vans or twitter feeds or old-fashioned word of mouth. I've never felt so helpless in my life.

"You're right, the police need more time. All we can do now is wait for them to get here."

CHAPTER THREE

Teddy

I hate waiting.

In my profession, people move. People go. People make snap decisions without thinking because sometimes those decisions determine the outcome of a long career or quick slide into obscurity. It's not that I have to be in charge; it's that if I don't think on my feet, people suffer. Dreams die. Livelihoods disappear. I've seen it once. I've seen it twice. I've seen it more times than I can count.

But I've never seen this.

Hearing her say, "*all we can do is wait*" bubbles across my skin like someone is dotting it with acid. I shift in place, contemplating. My heartbeat quickens with anticipation, my fingers itch to punch something, my shoulder brushes against her breast in ways that would normally find me leading her to a bed.

Right now, this chick could strip naked in front of me, and I wouldn't be at all interested. There's too much adrenaline pumping through my brain for the leftover endorphins to go anywhere else.

I don't like to wait. I'm a doer. I'm not helpless.

"This is ridiculous," I finally whisper, making a move to stand up. "Maybe we should just go out there and—"

"No." Her hand grabs at my arm, and she squeezes hard, stopping my momentum. For the love of everything holy, her nails are sharp. I envision permanent half-moon shapes in a row across my left bicep, and not for a good reason.

But good reason or not, my adrenaline rush fizzles. She's scared; despite the bravado, despite this being her job. I can hear the fear in her voice. She's here to keep me safe, and is keeping that promise at all costs. Someone needs to keep her safe in return. In this second, that someone is me.

"I locked the door, remember? No one's going out there but me," she says. "I'm the one with the gun, and it's my job to keep you safe."

She has a gun? So much for feeling like a hero.

"You have a gun?"

"I work security. Of course, I have a gun. How else would I keep you secure?"

"That's legal?"

"It is in Washington, if you have a special license. I do."

Okay, fair enough, but the thought never crossed my mind. Guns make me uncomfortable and relieved at the same time. Considering we're in such close quarters, I'm not sure which emotion is more predominant at the moment. If the shooter opens the door, you bet your life I'll feel relieved. If it accidentally goes off in my direction, I think the answer to that is an obvious one.

"Is it loaded?" I ask.

"Yes, but the safety is on. There's no danger of it accidentally going off, if that's what you're worried about." She pauses. "Not all of us carry them, but thanks to psychopaths like this guy, some of us do. Believe me, I'm not really happy about it either." She sighs. "I can holster it if you want me to."

I swallow. I want her to, but I feel ridiculous saying it. I've been around guns before—at the shooting range, my dad took me hunting a couple times as a kid—but this one is designed specifically for shooting humans, at least in this situation. I'd rather not have that human be me, not out there or in this room. Still, I have no idea how to respond.

Turns out, I don't have to. I hear it slip into place and snap closed.

"There. It's aimed at the wall and away from you, so stay on this side of the room. But I'll warn you, if I have a reason to use it, I will. And I won't stop to ask permission."

She's a badass with a no-nonsense voice. I like it a little more than I should.

"If you need to use it, be my guest," I say, sitting up and settling against the wall again. "I just hope it doesn't come down to that. And please don't accidentally aim it at me."

"You and me both, and I won't," she says, scooting next to me. Her presence immediately makes me feel more secure, less alone. "And for the record, neither of us is opening the door right now. My job is to protect you, and that is what I'm doing. Besides, there could be more than one person shooting. I doubt it, but it's possible. I would never live with myself if you got hurt on my watch. So don't make any stupid moves toward the door again. Got it?"

Dang. This chick is tough, and I wouldn't dream of arguing with her. I press my back against the wall and sigh, settling in when her shoulder brushes against mine. Just when I once again begin to feel comfortable, a gunshot blasts through the arena.

The sound of exploding glass rains around us, loud even inside this room.

The lights. He must have aimed for the spotlights.

The same hysterical voice shouts orders.

"Get on the floor now!"

A mass of people scream.

The gun goes off again, and I dive to the floor.

Bringing the still-nameless girl with me. Bodyguard or not, I'm a man, and she's a woman, and I was raised to be a gentleman. Call me sexist if you want to, but anyone who does can shove it up their ass.

She buries her head underneath me, her body shaking everywhere...putting a few cracks in all that bravado. If she wants to take care of me, she can. But I'll do the same for her. She's not the only one who doesn't ask permission.

———

Jane

I've been underneath him for several seconds, and I'm silently praying he doesn't move. I'm supposed to be tough, but right now, I'm terrified. The screams have subsided, but I can still hear them in my mind. How many people are dead?

I've never cried on the job, and I won't cry now, but a single tear manages to escape. Crying is a private thing for me. The kind of private that can have me sobbing uncontrollably in a dark bathroom one minute and walking out as if nothing ever happened the next. Emotions run deep inside me, deep deep, yet most people never see anything but my smile. It isn't the way I like it, but it's what I'm used to. For twenty-seven years, it's been the outward disguise that keeps me safe.

The irony of the moment isn't lost on me. So much for safety.

I sniff into his shoulder. He must take it as a sign to move because he shifts—first one leg, then another. And then he's off me, and I'm aware that the make-up I've worn since six-thirty this morning is more than likely lying in a puddle underneath my head. I swipe at my eyes just in case the lights come back on. It's black as night in here, but I'm still embarrassed. Bodyguards shouldn't cry, not ever and particularly not in front of the person they're trying to protect. For one second, I consider apologizing, but then I don't. This isn't the time for wasted pleasantries. For someone I just met, he's already seen me at my worst.

Hold your head up, Jane. And look people in the eye. And for heaven's sake, smile. Little girls should never be without a smile. Don't you want people to think you're pretty?

My mother's well-intentioned but misguided voice echoes from a hollow place in my past. A place that knows smiles don't fix things, and pretty isn't always an asset.

I sit up, but Teddy doesn't let go of my arm. For that, I am thankful. All that trying not to cry has left my throat raw. All that worrying about my make-up has left me feeling shallow. I feel around for the water bottles and open one. The water is warm, but that hardly matters. It quenches the burn, and I swallow half the bottle in three quick gulps. Only then does it occur to me to offer Teddy one.

"I hope you don't mind that I took your water. Want one?"

A single breathy laugh escapes his lips. "Maybe later. And for the rest of our stay, my water is your water."

"You make it sound like we're at a hotel." I regret the words the second I say them.

"I'd give anything for that to be true." I know he means he would like to be out of this situation—not that he would want to be at a hotel with me. But still, I feel myself blush.

"Same." An uncomfortable silence descends. One that has me questioning his earlier meaning. Best to ignore it and change direction.

"I'm sorry about the tears." I nod toward the floor and

run a finger under both eyes. "Normally, I'm not that emotional."

In public.

He scoots a little closer until our shoulders are pressed together, his hand still on my arm. It's something I've quickly discovered about Teddy Hayes. He likes close contact. Maybe only when he's in danger, but there hasn't been a moment inside this closest when he hasn't been touching me somewhere.

"I don't know about you," he says, "but normally people aren't shooting at me. I'd cry too, if I remembered how." My heart pinches. Something in that statement speaks of a sad past, but I don't have time to decipher it.

The sound of footsteps outside the door makes us both freeze. My breathing stops, and his breathing stops, and time marches backward and forward and upright and upside down and then settles five seconds later with a resumed tick-tock-tick of the seconds. I feel around for my gun, but release it when the footsteps recede. Farther. Farther. Gone. I return the gun to its spot against the wall and breathe deeply as we settle next to each other again. I understand it now, his need to remain in close contact. I press into him a little further. The desire for human connection has never been more intense than in these last few minutes. It's what keeps me feeling a little more like a valuable commodity, and a little less like a moving target.

And I need to feel human.

"What's your name?" he whispers.

"My name?"

"Yes. You already know mine. I think I should know yours just...just in case."

In case something happens, he means. In case we don't come away from this and I'm the last person he ever talks to.

Panic loosens its fist around my lungs while dread unfurls

itself in my gut. Two very distinct emotions engaged in a war of extremes. My teeth begin to chatter, but I take a deep breath and give him what he wants. It's the least I can do.

"It's Jane. My name is Jane."

———

Teddy

Jane.

Her name is Jane, and it takes everything in me not to utter something like a gasp of unbelief, or a protest that her name can't be Jane. It can't. No one names their kid Jane anymore. No one thinks of the name Jane. It's plain. It's the author of seventeenth-century literature. It's common. No one likes the name Jane.

Except me.

Since I was fourteen and had a vivid dream that I'd married a blonde girl named Jane. I've secretly been looking for her ever since. I never told anyone about it.

What are the odds I would find her here?

Hope surges and crashes at the exact same time.

CHAPTER FOUR

Jane

He hates my name, which makes no sense. Because even though it's boring and I've never met anyone with the same name as mine, unless television characters and ancient book heroines count, it's not *that* bad. Still, I heard the low *'huh?'* when he whispered it, even if the reaction was brief.

"What's wrong with Jane?"

"What?" His hand flinches as though I've surprised him, but I don't wait for an answer before I decide to give him another reason to grimace.

"I was just being nice earlier. Teddy isn't that great either, you know. I'm not sure what it means, but it's probably something awful like *full of oneself* or *thinks he is God's gift to women* or—"

"It means God's gift," he says, interrupting me.

"What?"

"Teddy. It means '*God's gift.*'"

"Are you serious?"

"Yep. But go ahead and finish what you were saying."

I blink and darn it, I have nothing. If my train of thought was heading somewhere, it just derailed over a steep mountainside and landed in a heap in the lowest part of the valley.

"Figures." It's all I come up with.

The edge of his shoe bumps against mine. "Just so you know, I happen to love the name Jane. Have since I was a kid."

Despite fear squeezing nearly all emotion from me, my heart gives a barely perceptible thud. Except for my mother, little old ladies, and literature buffs, no one's ever loved my name. Plain Jane was my nickname all through school, even when I was winning childhood beauty pageants. *Smile pretty, Jane. No one likes a frown.* Probably the reason my classmates came up with the nickname in the first place. That kind of confused insecurity sticks with you.

"Don't patronize me. No one likes my name."

"I don't say things I don't mean," he says. "For your information, back when I was fourteen I—"

We hear it at the same time. A siren. The *it* turns into a *them* all at once when one siren is followed by another and another and another. Doors slam. Men yell. A bullhorn blasts. A gunshot. Another. A Law and Order episode is happening outside the room.

Our breaths mingle as Teddy looks at me, and I look at him. I know he's looking at me because I feel it all around us.

This is good.

This is bad.

Maybe it's both.

———

Teddy

I'm worried, but I refuse to show it. If I were alone in this room, they might find me crouching in a corner, trying to get away from the sound of bullets and screaming, but with Jane in here with me, I refuse to let myself feel anything but fierce determination.

The plan works until her cell phone rings.

We have service!

The vibration cuts through my bravado like the sound of the police bullhorn that echoed only seconds ago—the blast reminiscent of a protester waxing poetic in the middle of a reverent prayer service. I dive to answer it, she dives to answer it, both of us crashing against each other in a frantic hope to connect with the outside world. Maybe it's her mother. I wish it were mine.

She reaches it first, only to fumble and send it clattering loudly across the concrete floor. By the time I blindly locate it, the ringing stops. I put the phone on silent, then hold it out toward her. Both of us are winded. Both of us are disoriented. My temple hurts from slamming into some part of her body in the darkness. Maybe her shoulder, maybe her shoe.

Her phone's battery is at four percent.

Blood rushes between my ears as I wait for it to ring again, or for us to be discovered. That drop was loud. Sweat collects on my upper lip. I'm cold and hot, clammy in the spots where all my joints connect. After a few harrowing moments, there's still no sound of approaching footsteps. I slump against the wall on a relieved breath. Maybe the sirens drowned out the noise, but we're safe. Things are deathly silent on the other side of this door, way too silent for a room filled with so many people.

"Who was it?"

I can feel it, the way her body winds itself so tightly she could spring on me and everyone else. Body rigid, eyes sharp, hand squeezing mine in a death grip, breathing shallow. She skips right over my question.

"Do you think anyone heard it ring?"

She can't keep the quake from her voice. I shake my head, hoping to convince her. If anyone heard it, if this ends badly and we're discovered in this room, I can't have her thinking she was at fault. Even if it was her phone.

"No, I don't. I think the sirens covered up the sound. Who was it?"

"My mother. She calls every Thursday night around this time. It won't take her long to start worrying, especially if I don't call back. She hates my job. Tells me so every time we talk."

Understandable, though I don't voice it. My mother hates my job as well, even though it already paid for her house. She's constantly worried I'll be the target of some obsessed fan. The jury's still out on what exactly motivated everything tonight. If the news has broken, there are probably twenty texts from her on my phone already.

I can't think of my mother's worry right now. "Can you text instead? She won't be able to hear you whispering."

"Good idea." Her voice shakes. She's terrified even though she's doing a heck of a job covering it up. She's one of those people who masks negative emotions with quick wit and biting words. I know what the disguise looks like. I wear it myself.

"Now that the police are here, maybe she will have heard something. The news will be national pretty soon, and it might be better for her to hear it from you."

"Okay, but I don't have much battery left."

"Type fast. See if she knows anything."

She comes to life and her fingers start tapping. If hope could be expressed in the tapping of letters, it would be shooting out her fingers in rainbows. I read over her shoulder and slowly watch the colors fade into nothing. A few minutes later, Jane sighs and sets her phone on her lap. I'm as discouraged as she is.

Her mother knew nothing, but is now scared to death. And curse of all curses, Jane's phone dropped to one percent during the exchange. We can't afford to use it again. Now we have no way to contact anyone, a feeling more dire than being locked inside this closet. That's what this night has done—spiraled straight to hell on a magic carpet complete with scorch marks around the edges.

I reach for a water bottle and drain it at once just to have something to do.

All I wanted to do was perform tonight, answer whatever texts had come through from Dillon, then climb on the tour bus, crack open a beer, and watch whatever was left of the Predators game on television. I bristle at my naivety. This job may have cost me everything—my safety, my freedom, quite possibly my life and the lives of a whole lot of innocent people. No wonder my mother hates it.

Like I said, straight to freaking hell.

I release a sigh and settle in next to G.I. Jane—it's my secret nickname for her—needing to feel the warmth of her body next to me. Needing an escape from the darkness. Needing to feel something other than terror. Maybe I've been too forward in keeping my hand on her shoulder, or my leg against her leg, but knowing I'm not alone makes this situation a bit more bearable. Even at this moment, it's all I can do to keep myself from reaching for her hand.

"We're going to make it out of here, Jane. The police are here and they're going to rescue us." I look at her even though I can't make out her features. I imagine no-nonsense, mousy brown hair, dark eyes, tanned skin, muscular arms and legs—maybe too muscular—and a tough-to-crack veneer despite the earlier tears. I may have the picture all wrong, but the only thing I remember seeing before she dragged me in here was a flash of her neck when she shoved me inside. The rest is fabricated from an old Demi Moore movie I remember seeing as a kid; the one where she shaved her head and wore thin, white tank tops. Is Jane wearing camo pants? Is her hair buzzed around the ears? I can't remember that, either. "Thank you for dragging me in here. I'm not sure where I would be if you hadn't pulled me from the crane." I stop talking, stuck on remembering how helpless I felt suspended in the air.

"I'm not scared of much," she surprises me by saying. "Not heights. Not spiders. Not confined spaces. Not strangers. Not guns. But tonight, I discovered that I'm terrified of being hunted. I know that sounds stupid since it's my job to protect people. I always imagined that would involve throwing myself in front of a crazed fan or even taking a bullet to the chest if necessary. I never fathomed it would involve hiding in a closet while a crazed lunatic shot into the crowd on purpose. What is wrong with people? Of course, I've seen this sort of thing on the news, but this is something I never thought would happen to me. It was hard not to just take off running."

I wait for her to gather her thoughts. Some people speak eloquently—in long drawn out speeches accented with flowery words and forceful persuasions. Others speak the way they think—in starts and stops and sudden rewinds. Jane is the latter. It's interesting. More than that, it's sincere. Most unplanned, off-the-cuff things are, especially when delivered in words.

"What kind of person would I be if I hadn't pulled you off that crane? I know it was—and still is—my job to protect you, but I wish I could have done more. Grabbed another person or two. Yelled for others to follow me."

I don't know what to say, how to assuage the unnecessary guilt she's feeling. It's understandable, but I say the only thing

I can think of. "Who knows, maybe before this is all over, we'll have the chance. And now that the police are here, hopefully this will be over soon."

I lean my head against the wall and blink up at blackness. From the moment we heard the first siren, I've been praying for this to end.

CHAPTER FIVE

Jane

A typical episode of Law and Order goes like this: the show opens, and life for the main character is normal and routine. Maybe he's a nine to five banker. Maybe she's a stay-at-home mom who works part-time at the local library. Ten minutes later, the first hint of danger appears in the form of gloomy theme music. Da-dum. Da-dum. At the half-hour mark, the banker slash librarian is dead, and cops are closing in on the bad guys. Twenty minutes later, all is well and viewers are engrossed in the happily ever after, while at the same time watching in silent victory as justice is served.

A trial commences.

The bad guys go to jail.

Detectives celebrate over a few rounds of beer at the local bar.

Screen fades.

Show over.

In real life, we've been sitting here for minutes, and nothing at all has happened. The sirens indicated hope, but that was it for our rescue. No front door has crashed open, no

shouting has commenced as the cops take down the bad guy.
No cheers of gratitude have gone up from the hostages. No
one has walked back here to tell us we can come out of hiding
and head home.

With every second that goes by, my spirits sink a little
lower and my mood grows a little darker. But that isn't the
worst of it. Not even close.

The shooter has gone silent. My mind screams. With
every second of not knowing, my imagination grows. I expect
the door to fly open and bullets to rain down on us, both of
us wounded or dead by morning. I don't like to imagine
myself dying. An overactive thought process doesn't pair well
with tight and tense limbs. My head hurts from all the thinking. My neck aches from all the straining. My jaw hurts from
all the clenching. But nothing hurts as bad as my heart. A
mental image of splayed and dead bodies—those outside and
my own in here— haunts me like I've never been haunted
before. With every breath, Teddy squeezes my hand tighter.
Where are the police? How long will it take them to make a
move? Worse still, will he hurt anyone else before they finally
take him down? How many more people will have to die?

It's brought me face-to-face with my own mortality, and I
don't much like the view.

I haven't been on the best terms with God in the last few
years, not since my parents divorced. My dad—the stricter
parent who made sure my butt was in a Methodist pew every
Sunday I spent at his house—remarried and moved to Idaho.
Regret runs deep on a few private issues, and currently, mine
is that I should have rectified my God situation before today.

Unlike me, I'm sure my father's seven-year-old son has a
direct line to heaven by now. I bet he'll never find himself
shut inside a six by seven space with a stranger wondering if
today will be the last day he lives. Even if he does, he'll prob-

ably know exactly where he's going for eternity, and my dad will be right by his side the entire time.

I'll probably go straight from here to a two by eight box buried six feet under. The prospect is frightening, to say the least.

"Teddy?"

He rolls his head to the side, and I can feel his eyes on me through the blackness. This must be how the visually impaired experience life, and now I get it. They say when your vision is compromised, all your senses are heightened: sense of smell and hearing and taste and fear. I can feel everything Teddy does, even though I can't see any of it.

"What?" he whispers.

"Do you believe in God?"

"Stop it." The firmness of his words surprises me. "We're not going to die. I won't let it happen."

"I think you've got it wrong. I'm supposed to be the one protecting you, not the other way around. But do you? Believe in Him, I mean?"

"Yes, I do. But you're the one who has it wrong. You might have been hired to be my bodyguard, but I'll be damned if I go down without taking care of you. My momma didn't raise a coward. I have bodyguards for when I'm out in public to keep crazy people from attacking me. They've tried a few times. But bodyguards aren't for taking the fall when we're locked inside a closet together. We're on a level playing field now, sweetheart. Get used to it."

I should be offended by his term of endearment, especially considering I'm a woman and am quite certain he wouldn't say that to a man. But I'm not offended, I'm touched. Teddy Hayes doesn't consider himself more important than anyone else, no matter what the tabloids might want you to believe.

"Alright. As long as you remember that it's my gun in the corner, and I'll use it if I have to."

He squeezes my fingers. "Be my guest. Just remember to warn me before you shoot, so I'll have time to duck."

I don't respond, too sick at the thought. The only way I'll need my gun is if the shooter discovers us in here. If that happens, warning Teddy will be the last thing on my mind. Killing the shooter will be the first. But despite my certainty, it does make me wonder.

If I die today, where will I wind up?

"Jane?" Teddy whispers.

"What?"

"Yes, I believe in God. And just so you know, I've been praying this whole time that He'll take care of us."

I think about that, then relent. "Okay, I'll start doing it too."

And I do, even though I'm not quite sure what to say or if anyone is even listening. All I know for sure is this: There are high points in life, and there are low ones.

This is one of the lowest points I've ever experienced. We need all the help we can get.

———

Teddy

The problem with the kind of praying we're doing is that it's the silent kind. Worthwhile, but lonely. And way too quiet. I know Jane is mostly a stranger, but the only sound on the other side of this wall is a low buzz of movement I can't decipher—there's no yelling, no threats, even the sirens have gone silent, I'm assuming because police cars are now in the parking lot. The gunfire has ceased for the time being, every one of my muscles is on alert and wound tight, and if I don't have someone to talk to now, my mind might snap. Turns out hostage situations are better when faced with companionship and some semblance of sanity. It's a lesson I never wanted or needed, but am still unfortunately faced with.

"Are you okay? You haven't said anything in the last few minutes."

"I'm praying like you told me to."

"What are you saying?"

"To God?"

"Yes." Normally I would crack a joke—*"No, to Bruce Willis"*—but my sense of humor is currently nonfunctioning.

She sighs. "Pretty much *'please please please,'* and then multiply that times a thousand. I'm not sure how many pleases it takes for God to finally hear me."

I grin a little. Even to my wound-up brain, the image of G.I. Jane begging anyone, is cute. "I think the right answer is four hundred and seventy-two. I hope it works."

"Me too."

She nudges my knee with her own. It's the first time she's initiated contact even remotely, and it sends a little thud into my stomach. Apparently, parts of me still function just fine. Unlike oil and water, positive emotion and terror don't separate when mixed; turns out you can't survive one without searching for the other. Welcoming it, even.

"How long do you think it's been now?"

She's an authority in this situation, but she's also afraid. For every minute that passes, the fear becomes more prominent, like irrational stage fright just before a performance even with an Grammy sitting on the mantle at home.

"Six years. But in reality, I'm betting ten or fifteen minutes at most."

She shifts in place. I can hear her scratching her leg, picking at a fingernail, pulling at the strands of her hair. Fidgeting all over. I can't say I blame her. Her breathing grows more prominent, and she sniffs. Crying? Probably. My nerves rattle around, bouncing across my chest, across the floor, looking for a place to land. Finally, they settle on the top of her head.

She lowers her head to my shoulder without asking, without hesitation, like we've done this a hundred times before. Maybe we have. Nothing about it is romantic, but everything about it is familiar. For a long time, we sit that way in silence.

"Thank you for holding my hand."

It's simple, but my chest catches. I never cry, but my eyes begin to sting anyway.

"I won't let go." *Do not give up. You have to survive this,* is what I don't say.

"Please don't."

I weigh it before I do it. And then I just give in because time isn't guaranteed and who cares about propriety anyway? I rest my chin on her head and turn just a bit, so it feels an awful lot like we're holding each other. The only thing I'm really holding is her hand, but that changes when she snakes an arm around my waist and rests it above the waistband of my jeans. The guard and the guarded; what a picture we would make if the door opened now. *People* magazine would have a fit with this, considering last month I informed them I rarely date.

Of course, this isn't a date—if it were it would be the worst date in the history of dates—

but it sure as hell would look intimate in a photo. Let the paparazzi speculate. Jane has sacrificed her life to protect me, the least I can do is stay still and give her what she needs. What *I* need. Like it or not, this is helping. I keep my hand in hers and just let it be, her head on my shoulder and my chin on her head. Two people resting against a wall and taking companionship where they can get it. And right now, God knows we need it.

I've heard this sort of thing happens; it happened when Dillon and Liam were stranded on that island together. When faced with a possible end, all pretense strips away, and humans reach out for one another. It's when nothing matters but basic need, and isn't that what it comes down to? People spend all their lives chasing possessions and money and status, but in the end, what they desire most is to be seen. To matter. In the end, basic need is all anyone wants.

Maybe He hears prayers after all.

I'm suddenly overwhelmed with the need to lighten the moment to keep myself from doing something stupid, like kissing her. Or opening the door and taking the shooter down myself. I keep glancing at it, wondering what might happen if I flung it open and tried to end this once and for all.

"As long as we're in here, maybe we should play a game," I say, dragging my gaze away from the thin sliver of light under the door. "You know, do something to pass the time. I'm going crazy wondering what's happening out there, and I'd like to keep myself from making a big mistake."

"I'll play, but do not get any weird, heroic ideas." Her warning is wrapped in relief at the distraction.

"I'm full of weird ideas, but right now, I'll refrain. Ever played *Say It*?" I breathe in, out, silently commanding my heart rate to calm down.

"No?" She asks it like a cautious question. "How do you play?"

I keep my head on hers, her hand in mine, and talk into the blackness. "We ask each other questions, and the first person to refuse an answer loses."

She shrugs. "Okay, you go first."

"I need to think of one. Give me a second."

"This is your game. You should have had one ready." Footsteps skitter outside the door, and she squeezes my hand tighter, burying her face into my neck. I hate this hate this hate this. "Hurry up before the breakdown I'm about to have takes over," she whispers. I can feel her heart pounding into my arm, her hand shaking inside my own, so I think fast. Too fast.

"Bottom or top?" I blurt, immediately regretting it. I slam my eyes closed and bang my head against the wall a couple of times.

The room goes tense; it's offended on her behalf.

"I'm not answering that. Think of a different question or this game is over." She keeps her head on my shoulder, so I take that is a positive sign.

"Sorry, it was all I could think of under pressure."

Fear does odd things to your brain, occasionally demanding your mouth take part of the blame. Why on earth did I ask that question? For a long moment, Jane says nothing at all, likely thinking of ways to physically torture me without tipping anyone off to our whereabouts.

"Honestly, Teddy," she finally says, lifting her head to look at me. I feel her breath on my face. "You say you want to play a game to ease your anxiety, and then you go and ask a question like that. Is your anxiety eased, at least?"

"Nope. I'm afraid it's doubled now."

This makes her laugh quietly, but it sounds half-desperate as the absurdity of this evening rolls over her like a Mack truck. Soon I join her, even though nothing is funny. Clearly, our minds have cracked.

"Why are we laughing?" she asks. It's a valid question, one with an easy answer.

"Because the alternative is worse."

The laughter drains out of both of us almost instantly, and she sighs. She sits up a little, but her hand stays put. I wouldn't be able to let go if she tried. Her hand is the security blanket I gave up on my seventh birthday, reincarnated in female form.

"Okay, I'll try again. Rock music or country?"

She scoffs. "Rock for sure, though I'm not a big fan of either."

My head snaps back. *Not a big fan?* "So...you just hate talented musicians, or you have no taste?"

"I have taste. I just prefer classical music.. And maybe Elton John."

"Most eighty-year-old men prefer that too."

"I'll ignore that comment," she says. "Okay, my turn. Jennifer or Angelina?"

"Both at the same time."

"You're the worst."

I might think she was annoyed, but her head finds my shoulder again, and she still hasn't let go of my hand. There's light radiating from Jane, but I might be the only one who can see it in the darkness. It's solid, comforting.

I find it and don't look away.

CHAPTER SIX

Jane

Can women really have it all?

It was an easy question, but he still hasn't answered. We've been playing this game for a few minutes now, and every question has been easy. And he was right, it's made me feel a bit better. Less anxious, despite the constant fear and tension hovering like a third person in the room with us. For some reason, this question has stumped him. I need him to answer; too much silence might usher in unwelcome thoughts.

"Teddy, you're supposed to answer without thinking. It's your rule."

He emits a low growl and bumps his head against the wall. It's a light tap, so the sound doesn't make me nervous.

"No matter how I answer, you're going to be mad," he says.

He's said this three times, but it makes no sense, and it's also very presumptuous. One, he doesn't know me that well. Two, my temper isn't that quick. And three, even if I do get angry, I'm very good at hiding it. Better than most, if I had to venture a guess.

"No, I won't. I keep telling you that." Men. They never listen. It's a wonder the human race keeps multiplying with the choices women have in front of them. And sure, the choice in front of me is the twenty-third hottest thing in America with his faded blue jeans and shaggy hair and sexy voice, but still. He's as stubborn as they come. I've discovered that much in the short time we've played this game.

"Fine, I guess I'll go with no."

No?

He said *no?*

I feel my eyes narrow. "You're a jerk."

His face turns until it's only inches from mine. I can feel his breath on my lips. "I knew you'd get mad."

I press back into the wall. "Of course, I'm mad. It's sexist."

"No, it isn't. It's reality. For the record, men can't have it all either."

Oh. Well, that's a new take. "Why not? It seems both could have whatever they want as long as each steps up and pulls their weight."

"Except people rarely do. One winds up making the money while the other takes care of the house and kids and everything else that goes into having a family. Or—and this is the most common version—*both* make the money while only one still takes care of the house and the kids and the pets and everything else that comes with having a family. So I suppose the real answer is yes, women and men can have it all. But having it all usually comes with a price."

I bite my bottom lip because he has a point. "You speak from experience?"

He shrugs. "I have great parents, but the balance of power usually left my mother stressed out and tired. They're still together, though, and they seem pretty happy about it. Not everyone can say that, I guess."

"No, they can't." I can't. The resigned edge in my voice sounds personal, like I just handed Teddy a notebook and offered him the chance to flip through my list of Man Issues. There are enough to fill an entire notebook. I should have confronted them long ago, or at least cornered my mother and demanded answers about why she was content to let me walk through so many life experiences without care or counsel. This game was supposed to lighten the mood, but I pulled the shades and painted the walls black, so to speak.

"Anything you want to talk about?" he surprises me by saying. "Turns out, my schedule is freed up for the foreseeable future." There's so much sincerity in his words that I don't know what to do with it. But talking about something so personal will produce tears, and tears will produce an aching sadness, and the two combined will send me into a state I might not climb out of. Right now, I can't afford to take the risk. So I don't.

"Not really. Maybe later."

He nods. "Okay, later it is."

The room goes still as reality settles back in.

How much later is anyone's guess.

———

Teddy

It's odd how you can laugh and feel like you're losing it at the same time.

This game started as a way to pass the time, and it has. But it's been quiet outside this room for a long time. Too quiet. I don't like it.

Jane's stomach growls again. She's pressed her hand to it more times than I can count to try and muffle the sound, but

I hear it. Every time I hear it. There's nothing in this room but me, Jane, bottled water, and an outfit change that seems ridiculous and petty under the circumstances. Before tonight, I spent real time worrying about the thirty seconds I had to change shirts under here and grab some water; so much time worrying that we'd practiced it down to the second. What a colossal waste of brain space and priorities.

We've been in this room for less than half an hour, but I've aged a decade in the span. It's so quiet on the other side of this door that I'm starting to wonder if the standoff is over and we're the only two holdouts left. Like a bad rerun of Punk'd that will have all cameras pointing our direction when we open this door, all of America laughing at our idiocy. I simultaneously want to check and not check. The former is winning. My patience is not. I need out of this room. I want out now.

"How long do you think it's been since we heard anything?" It's an odd question, but it's the only way I can think to get to the point.

"I don't know. Maybe ten minutes. Why?"

My heart does a little flip at the direction my mind is taking, but I ignore it and focus on the matter at hand.

"I think we should open the door and see what's going on."

"It's locked."

"It's not like I can't unlock it."

"No." There's a threat inside her tone I don't like.

"Nothing bad will happen. The shooter won't even notice me. I'm not afraid of him."

"Then be afraid of me. I'll amend my statement. You're not going out there unless it's over my dead body. So if you really want to know what's going on, you'll have to send me out because it's the only way I'll let you find out."

I rake a hand over my face and stand up, careful to keep

my shoe touching hers. I don't want to lose contact with her in the darkness. "Jane, think about it. How long has it been since you heard a noise? A shout? A cry? Even any footsteps?"

"A while, but I'm not going to risk you getting shot. It's my job, remember? If anyone gets shot here, it's me."

A part of me dies at that visual, so I come at it from a new angle. "What if the standoff is over and we just don't know it? What if they've already apprehended the shooter and we're just sitting here like a couple of morons? No one even knows we're here. They've probably forgotten all about us, and we don't have a working phone to find out."

If the lights were on, there's a hundred percent chance I would see her leveling me a look. Even I can hear the crazy in my words.

"You think they've forgotten about you," she deadpans. "You think they all just left, turned off the lights, and went home. You honestly think they won't be combing every inch of this arena when this is over to make sure you're unharmed?" She huffs as hard as one can while whispering. "Me, they'll forget about. You, not a chance."

Another statement that pings my heart. She's right; the world will forget about her. Most people in this arena would step over her to get to me, and I know it. But I won't. Not ever. It isn't every day that someone literally puts their life at risk for you. Especially a stranger.

"Alright, forget it. It was a dumb idea, anyway."

"Yes, it was."

We're sitting side-by-side, shoulder to shoulder in the dark. So it surprises me when I feel her elbow nudge me aside with a light jab to the ribs.

"Fine, I'll try to open the door. But you stay here just in case, do you understand?"

"Jane, come on—"

"I'm not arguing with you. Stay there or no deal. Agree to it or—"

It's then that her walkie crackles to life. After minutes of it lying useless and presumably dead on the floor, we both jump from the sound.

The sound of a male voice comes through the receiver, hard to hear because he's speaking in a whisper that barely registers.

"Jane, give me your location."

"Andy!" Jane lunges for the walkie. I don't know who Andy is, but he just became my new hero. Right behind Jane.

"Andy, are you okay?" she whispers back while relief floods parts of me I never knew I possessed. Isolation is a terrible feeling, and this guy just tossed us a net. It might turn out to be filled with holes, but at least it's something. "I have Teddy Hayes with me underneath the stage, and we're both alright." I hear it now, the way she wipes tears from her face as they leak down her skin. My hand wraps around her arm, and I lean in to listen.

"I'm fine, but stay there," Andy says. "Police have the suspect confined to a small section of the arena, but he still has a few hostages. Everyone else has been evacuated, but the power is out, and they want you to stay put until he's apprehended. I think he might have been after Teddy specifically. I'll come get you when they give us the all-clear. Might be a while, though. Again, don't move."

She nods vigorously while my heart descends straight into my shoes. *After me specifically.* Now it's confirmed: this entire thing is my fault.

"We'll stay," she assures him.

"Who is he?" I say into the walkie, desperate to know. "Why was he after me? And how many people were hurt?"

"Teddy..."

I shake my head. Jane's concern won't trump my need to

know. Thankfully Andy complies. His answer comes through loud and clear, though I soon wish it hadn't.

"A man, looks to be middle-aged. And a lot of people are hurt. Just stay in the room, and we'll talk about it after I come get you. And Teddy?"

"What?" I grip the walkie, wanting some sort of assurance I know he can't give.

"He was in it for the notoriety, for the fame of targeting a musician, nothing more. These kinds of people are sick and can't be rationalized with."

"Okay." His words are meant to help, but they don't. Any way you look at it, if I didn't exist, this situation wouldn't either. Teddy Hayes, one of *People Magazine's* Sexiest Men Alive. Teddy Hayes, unwilling participant in the murder of innocents.

I back away and let Jane finish the conversation, my limbs and shoulders heavier than they've ever been.

What drives people to do this, and why?

I'm the first to know life is hard, but I can't imagine dragging innocent people into my madness with me. Nothing in life could possibly be that bad.

———

I hear the rattle of the door handle before I register what's happening.

"You're still going to open the door?" I ask, looking up into a face I can't even see. As curious as I was to open it a few moments ago, now I'm desperate to stay hidden behind it. Someone is out to kill me, and I don't want to be found. It's the biggest catch-twenty-two I've faced in life, and I resent it. It makes me feel as much like a survivor as a coward.

"Sit down against the wall. And be still while I grab my gun."

"Jane, what are you doing?" I slide the gun toward her, careful to keep it on the floor and pointed away from me.

"I'm opening the door to get a look at things. And then I'll close it. It'll take two seconds, tops."

I hear the rustle of leather, the click of a belt, and the cock of a weapon. Every bit of it fills me with a dread I may never be able to shake.

"Ready?"

"No," I whisper, my head lowering to my hands.

I hear a few clicks and jiggles of the door handle, and then Jane cracks the door. Nothing but silence greets us, so she opens it a bit wider. I can't help myself; I look up at the last second.

A man in white shoes is the first thing I see.

Then I see everything else.

My blood freezes.

My vision swims.

I'm under the stage with Teddy, Jane told Andy earlier.

She didn't say we were under the walkway.

She didn't tell him we're at the opposite end of the real stage.

He didn't realize the section the shooter is confined to...

is ours.

CHAPTER SEVEN

Jane

I quietly close the door as Teddy gasps for air behind me.

If the shooter had turned even a few inches, he would have spotted us.

Even though he didn't, it still takes effort not to sob at the reality of our situation.

I squeeze my eyes closed and cover my mouth with one hand, desperate to erase the memory of what I just saw, and frantic not to let the anguish of it leak out. I can't manage either, so I sink to the floor instead. The gun in my hand feels like poison, so I slowly lower it. Careful to reengage the safety. Careful to slip it inside the holster. Suddenly I don't want to touch the thing.

I cry without tears.

I cry without noise.

I cry from a place that's dry and desolate. A place filled with unbelief and terror. A place stacked with pain on pain on pain. That place only exists in the worst of circumstances, and I've never once visited. Not in my childhood, not when my dad left, not when he replaced me with a whole other family.

Even when I didn't have him, I still had my life. I can't say the same for everyone outside.

The arena looked both eerie and haunting, a fog-filled graveyard before sunup had a chance to clear the area of a heavy haze of fear. And the shoes. The sight of them right in front of us will forever haunt my dreams.

It's an easy section to barricade. I remember it, the way it snaked around the soundboard and computers, already cordoned off to keep the fans away from expensive, irreplaceable equipment. They're all right here. Closed in. Too close. The sight was almost too much to bear.

The fact that Teddy and I are still alive, still tucked safely in this room, puzzles me more than anything. This isn't the way things work in horror movies. I've seen enough to know the normal sequence of events. The low hum of foreboding music. The overhead lights that quit working at the worst possible time. The victim's clumsy fall that gives the bad guy time to catch up and overtake the helpless girl. The jab to the heart, the horrified scream, the rivers of blood, the chilling laugh...on to the next victim. The good guys always get hurt while the bad guys return in a sequel and begin the morbid events all over again.

We're right behind him.

Any minute now, he's bound to find us.

We wait a long time in shock, both of us breathing heavily, backs pressed against the wall as we sit in shock. Teddy's hand is once again wrapped firmly around mine while I squeeze back like our contact is the only thing standing between me and a bullet. Maybe it is. Maybe that's why I can't let go. Because letting go feels a lot like being alone, and alone is the last place I want to be right now. Terror snakes through my insides and coils around my lungs, but as long as I don't let go, I can convince myself that I'm safe. Cared for. Connected to another soul that I didn't even know earlier today.

Dying alone would be the worst kind of tragedy.

Having a partner in this nightmare is the best and most horrible gift.

"How long do you think this will take?" he asks so quietly I have to strain to hear him.

"I have no idea."

"Feels like an eternity already."

It feels like so much more. Like a lifetime lived in one night. *What ifs* keep playing in my mind like a dying man's last wish. What if had tried the exit door myself instead of relying on Andy? What if I had pulled my gun on the shooter and at least fired a single shot? What if I had more time?

I would do everything differently if I had more time.

I realize I've dozed off when my head falls forward, startling me awake. Sleep really is the best coping mechanism, though, as far as I know, Teddy hasn't slept at all. I slide myself upright and shake my head a little to clear it. I'm cold and sore from thirty minutes of tense muscles. What I wouldn't give to climb underneath my purple and brown down blanket at home and bury my head for days. It's what I plan to do the moment this ordeal is over. I'm known as a workaholic; sick days, vacation days, and personal days are piled around me like matchsticks because I'm always afraid to use them. Not after this. The second we get out of here, I'm cashing in my vacation days and taking time off. It's long past time to put my normal routine on hold.

The light on my phone comes on; Teddy studies it. The glow illuminates his face in the darkness, making his features clearer to see. He's a mess of tangled hair and downturned eyes and resignation. "It's almost nine."

My body sags against the wall. "So, we've been here nearly an hour."

"I guess so."

I imagine the gunman pacing outside the door, keeping tabs on stragglers, making sure no one has easy access to a working door. I imagine him busting down this door and pelting us with bullets. An overactive mind can often be a girl's worst enemy, even a girl trained to keep emotion out of her job.

Teddy turns off the phone and the room goes black once again, though I feel his eyes on me even in the blindness.

"My cousin wants me to be a bridesmaid in her wedding. The maid of honor, actually. It's in February." There are a hundred things I might have expected him to say, but this one catches me off guard.

"Excuse me, what?"

"Yep, maid of honor. That's the text she sent me right before I went on stage tonight. At first, I said no, but then I gave in when she promised me I wouldn't have to wear a dress."

"That might make for a nice headline." I know what he's doing. He's giving us something else to think about besides our grim reality. It's what we both need, and I'm grateful.

He sighs. "That's what I was afraid of. What it would look like if the press got a hold of the story? *Teddy Hayes In Drag*." He accents each word like one could imagine it written in lights. "Seems like such a stupid thing to worry about now, doesn't it?"

I shrug. "I don't know. I think we worry about a lot of things without realizing worse things are around the corner. Doesn't mean the original worry was stupid. A better conclusion might be that it's pointless to worry about anything. Today's worry becomes tomorrow's laughed-at dinner conversation. For the record, I worked your show tonight because a friend wanted floor tickets for her boyfriend because he couldn't afford them, so I applied for the job. And now I'm not sure 'friend' is the word she'll use to describe me after this."

He sucks in a breath and tightens his grip on my hand. "There's no way you could have known this would happen. But I'm sorry, Jane. You should be out there checking on him and not stuck in here watching over me."

"I'm not stuck, and I don't even know him. I'm exactly where I'm supposed to be. He's probably out now anyway. If I remember right, the tickets were on the opposite side of the stage. I won't be getting anyone else free tickets in the future, though. Not at all, and definitely not without giving them safety lessons first."

"There are safety lessons for this? How does one react when a madman has a gun?" There's not an ounce of sarcasm in his tone, so I tell him.

"First rule of safety if a shooter is in your midst: Get underneath something. A chair, a desk, a table. Anything that might protect you from a stray bullet or keep you out of the gunman's line of vision. Generally, if people can't see you, they forget about you."

"Out of sight, out of mind?"

"A worthless statement when it comes to romance, but it's a real thing in this scenario. The longer you can remain hidden, the better. Even if that means you have to keep moving to stay concealed."

"The second rule?"

"If you're able, hide close to an exit. That way, when the doors open—and sooner or later, they will open—you'll be one of the first to escape. I realize that sounds selfish in this sort of situation, but your own safety should be your primary concern. There are almost always casualties in these circum-stances, so try hard not to be one of them. And three, do not engage. No matter how tempting it might seem to play the hero, don't."

"Says the woman with her own gun."

"I'm trained for this, as are the police currently staked outside the building. Leave the heroics to us."

"So, you're saying I should shrink back and be a wimp?"

"Yep, if you want to survive."

"What if I don't like the way it looks for you to—"

"Protect you... because I'm a woman?"

He sighs. "Back to that, are we? No, I was going to say 'take the fall for me.' Call me a chauvinist pig if you must, but most men don't believe in hiding and letting a woman get shot for them. I respect you a little more than that. Also, I'm not weak or heartless."

"I appreciate that, I do. But letting me do my job isn't weak, not to me. So please don't do something stupid like get shot trying to prove a point. If you need a reason, think of my performance review. You don't want me to get fired, do you?"

He doesn't respond. So much silence descends on this tiny room, it would be easy to convince myself that he left. I wait. Then wait some more. When I can't take the quiet anymore, his whispering is the only thing keeping me sane.

"Teddy?"

"I'm here. Just thinking."

"About what?"

"That you're pretty amazing. I've known a lot of women in my life, but not one since high school has ever called me stupid."

At this, I laugh. "I have a secret for you, Teddy Hayes. I'm not like any other woman you've ever met."

I expect him to laugh back, but he doesn't. Instead, he gives my hand a squeeze, and we settle back against the wall.

———

Teddy

I didn't intend to fall asleep, but I didn't intend for a lot of things that have happened today. Sometimes you just roll with a situation and throw a tantrum after the fact.

A few minutes or hours or days later, I wake up to a raging headache and something pressing against my shoulder. My first instinct is to swat it off—it's a nuisance, it's uncomfortable. My second is to fight—maybe I've been caught, maybe I've been bound, maybe I'm already dead. My third—the instinct I develop in the two seconds it takes for my mind to become lucid—is to remain still. Jane's head is on my shoulder, and she's sound asleep.

Her hair—good lord—it smells like roses. It reminds me of my great-grandmother's flower garden that bloomed for twenty-eight straight years in the back corner of her two-acre downtown Nashville lot. Even though her home was surrounded by skyscrapers and miles and miles of oil-scented pavement, the stubborn woman refused to sell, saying she built that house with my great-grandfather, and if the city wanted it, they would have to tear it down with her still inside. I used to think keeping the home was a foolish decision on her part; I now see it as a testament to the strong will that kept her alive.

She died eight years ago this month. She was ninety-five. Her house has since been turned into a Denny's restaurant, the scent of bacon and grease a constant reminder of what used to be and is no more. The old flower bed became a foundation for two dumpsters and an oversized recycling bin. How's that for a family legacy?

The scent of Jane's hair brings all the memories rushing back. I remember her hair being short, or maybe it was pulled back. I remember blonde, although it could be red. In my mind, she is tough and no-nonsense, overly tall and muscular, not exactly pretty but not ugly either. Right, wrong, or in-between, men have perceptions of people in her line of work, the same perceptions they might have of a female body-builder or a cop. Not unattractive, but not soft and gentle either. The kind of woman who would literally carry the weight in a relationship.

The scent of her hair is shaking up my normally straight line of thinking and turning it into a web of mangled scribbles. If these are the last moments of my life, I suppose it's no wonder.

Why the heck am I thinking about relationships?

I wish I'd made time for one.

I've always thought relationships were for whipped, desperate romantics like Liam and Chad. Listening to those guys talk about love gives me pains in more places than my head. It's nauseating the way they wax poetic about missing their women, about being in love, about soulmates and life-long partnerships. I never know what I want for breakfast tomorrow, let alone for my whole life. As God is my witness, relationships aren't for me. I like casual. I like non-committal. I like one night stands and "don't forget your shoes on the way out." I like painless and uncomplicated. I like "you go your way, I'll go mine, no, I do not want your phone number."

I like the smell of roses.

I press two fingers to my temple to slow my ridiculous, out-of-nowhere, depression-ridden thoughts, and Jane shifts in place. Slowly I lower my hand as to not wake her up. The roses mix with cinnamon and the smallest hint of evergreen —no idea how that's possible underneath the stage of a fifteen-thousand seat arena, but here we are. I close my eyes and listen to her breathe. The scent of a woman is one of my favorite things. The scent of a tough one who could undoubt-edly take me down with the flick of her finger has me stifling a groan. I'd like to be taken down by her. Even here, even now.

My mind. It's a jumbled mess of thoughts spinning all sorts of weirdly inappropriate directions. Why am I even thinking about this? Worse, what if it's the last time I ever do?

I don't want my life to be over.

I don't want my last moments on earth to be lived on a closet floor with a woman I can't even see.

I thought I'd be old when my time was up; married once or twice with a few kids to complete the package. I never thought I'd be twenty-eight and on the upward slide of a very prolific career. How fair would it be for everything to stop now? And how am I going to get married a couple times when I've never really been in love? How awful am I to be thinking of myself when several outside are already hurt or...worse?

My chest feels tight. I think this might be what a panic attack feels like.

I take a deep breath to ease the grip it has on my throat, then plant a hand on my chest to make my heart rate slow. Neither work, but both cause Jane to stir.

"What's happening?" she whispers, half-asleep.

I guess the groan wasn't stifled like I thought.

"Nothing," I say. "Go back to sleep."

Her head sinks into my shoulder, and she curls into me. "Do you want me to move my head?"

"No," I say the word too quickly, but I want her to sleep. I want her to stop talking and sleep and stay put and give me something to think about besides thousands of frightened fans and one heartless man's cold-blooded ability to end lives so casually. God knows how many people he's cut down without regret or second thought. More could be on the horizon.

We could be two of them.

"Okay," she says with a sleepy sigh.

She's tired. Mind tired. Bone tired. The kind of tired that latches onto your organs and pumps through your blood, and has very little to do with lack of sleep. That same kind of tired is running through my veins at such a rapid pace that it might take over my cells as the only element keeping me alive.

Jane yawns and tucks herself further into my neck. I know she's more asleep than awake. I know she means nothing by it. But I wish I could wrap an arm around her waist and pull her closer as much for my sake as for hers. I've read about strangers clutching one another during plane crashes, and acquaintances kissing each other in workplace ambushes, and I've always, always thought it was crazy. Now I get it. If Jane weren't in this room—if I were here alone—I don't know how I would make it through this ordeal intact. She's keeping me sane. She's the only thing stopping me from doing something foolish. *"Don't be a hero,"* she said. It's only because she's here that I'm choosing to follow her advice.

"I'm so tired. Just gonna sleep a little longer." A single drop of water that hits my sleeve and seeps through the black cotton fabric has me sucking in a breath. She's been crying, probably cried herself to sleep without me noticing. The reality of it sends a small but very prominent crack through the middle of my heart. She may be tough, but she's not hard.

Without thinking, I bring my hand around her back and pull at her waist. She fits nicely into my side, this girl named Jane that I've known only a handful of hours. I still can't believe it's her name.

"I'll wake you if anything happens." The words are a breath, a line spoken to someone on the cusp of a dream, and then she's asleep again. She grows so relaxed that I begin to drift. I fight it for a second, and then let sleep pull me under. It isn't difficult to move Jane's head to my chest. It isn't difficult to shift positions until I'm lying on the floor, one arm around her waist, the other resting on the top of her head-.Her hair is definitely pulled up into a tight bun. I finger it, finding comfort in the strands. One has escaped, and it becomes my plaything. Her hair is curly, or at least it feels that way in the dark.

Sure, we're strangers.

Sure, we're nothing more than acquaintances.

But this is our trauma, and going through it with someone sure beats going through it alone.

CHAPTER EIGHT

Jane

I wake up on Teddy's chest, and just so we're clear, lying on the floor is a terrible way to sleep.

To save myself the embarrassment of him finding me this way, I gently roll off and curl on my left side on the hard concrete. Everything hurts—my back, my shoulders, my head from crying myself to sleep, my hair from this tight bun I've worn since noon. I pull out pins and an elastic and let my hair fall down my back, sighing in relief right along with my scalp.

But despite my aching everything, nothing hurts as much as my mouth. I reach for a water bottle in the dark and drain it, feeling marginally better but still awful.

The heat in this room is oppressive. It's the middle of November, and it feels like August during a rare Southern-fed heatwave. Muggy. Sticky. Soggy. I'm wearing tight black pants, a white button-up, and a jacket I should have ripped off when we first locked ourselves in here. I slide it off my shoulders right along with the button-up. I've never been as thankful for the tank top rule as I am now. "No visible underthings" is an actual regulation of the job. At first, I thought it was sexist

—now I don't care. I ball up the jacket and shirt and use them as a pillow, blinking up at blackness while I listen to Teddy breathe.

There are no vents to help circulate air. The atmosphere is stale, ventilation is non-existent, everything smells musty, and supplies are limited.

And nothing at all is happening. Maybe the suspect has already been apprehended. Maybe Andy will call any second to tell us we can leave.

"Jane? You okay?" His voice is a low hum. I turn toward the sound.

"I thought you were asleep."

"It's too hot to sleep."

"I think I've lost five pounds from sweat alone."

"Gross."

"I agree."

He scoots a little closer, pressing his forearm against mine, always seeking, always touching. "I dreamed I was swimming in my parent's back yard pool, and for some reason, I was wearing my football uniform from high school. I was drinking pool water through a straw, and when I couldn't get it down fast enough, I went under and started gulping. My mother was yelling at me to stop, but I couldn't. And then I couldn't swim back up because my uniform was too heavy, so I panicked. And now my stomach hurts even though it was only a dream. I wish I knew what it meant."

"You played football in high school?"

"In theory, though. I spent every game standing on the sidelines. I was five feet five inches tall on graduation day if I was standing up straight. Also, I was drowning in the dream, if you're interested in that part."

I manage a smile. "Please don't drown. But I think the most important part of that dream is that you felt powerless, and that feeling made you panic. Not all that hard to figure out under the circumstances."

"What are you, a dream whisperer?"

"It's my side job. On Saturdays, I tell fortunes at traveling carnivals in Texas."

"Just Texas? Because you might make decent money in New York or LA."

"Just Texas now, but I'm thinking about expanding."

"Thank God. I'd hate to see that side business stagnate."

"It'd be a shame considering I interpret dreams correctly almost half the time."

"You must be in high demand with those statistics."

"I have a stack of singles you'd be jealous of."

"From fortune-telling, or are the singles from your *other* side job?"

"I work that one only on Wednesdays."

"Why just Wednesdays?"

"Because it's half-price drink night, and the men at the bar get too drunk to care what anyone looks like."

"Well, granted, I haven't seen your face, but I would think it'd be good enough for the occasional Thursday as well."

"With compliments like that, no wonder you have groupies lined up."

"You're welcome."

"I didn't say thank you."

His quiet laugh turns into a sigh we both share. Silly banter is odd when spoken with the weight of unease, like telling a joke when the crowd already knows the punch line. Polite laughter, strained smiles, a pitter-patter of applause. Is this horrendous night almost over? Nothing about it is funny. "It's been quiet for a long time. Do you think we should—?" Teddy abruptly sits up, and my stomach falls. Even in the darkness, I know this move, this stance. He's determined. I don't like it.

"No," I say it hard like I mean it. I sit up beside him.

"No, what?"

"We're not opening the door again."

"Jane, it's been too long, and we need to know what's going on. You know it, and I know it. It will only take me a second to—"

When the light from my cell phone comes on, he stops talking. "It's been forty-five minutes since last time. It isn't smart, Teddy," I say, but it's weak. I set the phone down in defeat.

"Forty-five, that's all?"

My shoulders sag. "That's all. It's not even ten o'clock yet." How can so little time pass while your spirit personally ages five years?

Still, I'm starting to cave because I'm losing my mind, and the idea of cracking the door one more time for a quick update seems less and less foolish. For a long minute, we sit in what feels like a sightless stare-down, him looking at me and me looking at him and both of us reflecting on projected outcomes. Will we get caught? Will we be discovered? Will we get shot?

"Give me a better idea then," he says.

I don't have a better idea, and that's the problem. My mouth opens in search of one, but nothing comes out. I have nothing to offer because he's right. We can't just sit here forever, but what are the options? Defeat is a heavy weight to bear when you're also the one holding the armor.

"Fine, sit back against the wall again." My voice wobbles on the foolish demand, but I can't help it. If I get caught, this whole thing could be over, and not in a good way. Yes, the shooter may be in this for the notoriety, but Andy already made it clear he's also targeting Teddy himself.

He can't get hurt. At this point, it would break me.

"No, let me do it this time."

"We're not having this conversation again. Back against the wall."

"Jane..."

"Now." I'm a very reasonable woman when I'm not working.

He hesitates. When I think he's about to move, I feel his hands on my shoulders, and he gives a squeeze. I think that's it, that he's going to move away, but Teddy surprises me and pulls me to him. He doesn't want to risk this any more than I do.

"Just take a look and close the door." He sighs into my hair, the kind of resigned sigh that leaves my spine prickled with both fear and something else I don't want to name. He smells good, he feels strong. For now, I'm safe and protected. It's a nice thing to have the tables turned for a moment. "Hey, you have long hair." This isn't what I expected him to say, and I smile-frown into the darkness.

"Did you think I had a buzz cut?"

"I may have at one point."

"At one point, when?"

"All the way until a minute ago."

"Nice to know the female bodyguard stereotype is alive and well."

"Nice to know I've been proven wrong. Say a quick prayer, okay?" He whispers the words into my ear, and my eyes begin to sting. I nod in a wordless promise. I've never been the praying kind—at least not in many years—but I am now. I'm not sure if God likes eloquence in conversation or if He's okay with short, pleading words, but fear is knotting my throat. All I can manage is a successive string of *please God please Gods* and right then and there I decide He'll accept it as my best. I'll work on expressiveness later when I'm safely out of this mess.

I open the door and my lungs close.

The moment of truth, but right now, I'd rather live a lie.

———————

Teddy

Jane has been quiet since she opened the door.

She closed it right away, so fast I didn't have a chance to see anything at all.

Even now, she's silent, though I've tried more than once to get her to talk. Finally, she takes a deep breath. I foolishly dare to hope it's to give me a real response.

"Do you have any pets, Teddy? That's my next question in the game."

"I don't want to play the game. Tell me what you saw."

"Nothing but people. Lots of people. Now answer the question."

I hesitate, but then relent. "If I told you I have three cats, would you think less of me?"

"Yes."

"Cool. Now it's my turn. What did you see?"

"Only yes or no questions, that's your rule."

"Fine. Did you see a gun? People? The police?"

"Yes to the people. My turn."

She's leaving something out, I can feel it. Something important. My heart begins to hammer like it hasn't in an hour.

"Jane."

"I asked you a question, Teddy."

"What question?" I can't hear anything over the throbbing in my throat.

"I asked if you like singing or songwriting better."

"Songwriting."

"Hash browns or French fries?"

"Hash browns. That's not even a contest."

It's a word volley. Hot potato. Don't let the ball drop or you'll lose the game. Don't get burned or you'll be scarred for life. I swallow.

"Christmas or—"

There's a thud against the door.

And another one.

"What did you see, Jane?"

My voice is too loud. My pulse is too hard. My blood is too cold.

"It isn't what I saw." Her voice cracks on the upward lilt. She's talking too loud. "It's who saw me."

"Who saw you?" I give her shoulder a little shake. Not too rough, but not too gentle, either. I should be shaking myself. Punching, even. I'm the one who wanted to open the door.

There's a gunshot. And another.

We scramble backward.

I hear the click of Jane's gun as the door slowly opens.

CHAPTER NINE

Jane

The boy who pushed his way in here...I'm not sure he's going to make it.

With the low glow of my phone's flashlight hovering overhead, I bend over the boy's prone body, my hair falling on his chest as I listen to his ragged breathing. His lungs are wet, his breaths spongy and thick. He came in whispering, shaking, pleading, covered in blood from his left shoulder to his forearm, soaked with urine on one side of his jeans. He collapsed in a heap the moment the door closed. I caught him in my arms just before he hit the floor. He's moaned off and on since, but he hasn't woken up.

A cut, deep and lacerating, trickles a thin stream of blood littered with tiny and not so tiny shards of glass. Thick glass. Spotlight glass. I remember hearing it rain down way too many hours ago, never once thinking about the people it was lightly impaling. The largest piece of glass was wedged in his skin at the bend of his elbow. Teddy pulled, and it ejected with a jerk, the backed-up blood flowing down to the boy's fingertips. All we've managed to do so far is to ebb the flow a bit. Hopefully, it's enough.

"How's his heart?" Teddy asks.

I bend closer to his chest to listen for a heartbeat. It's still there, seemingly strong as ever. But without a stethoscope or a blood pressure cuff, I'm just guessing.

"Still beating steadily." That much I know.

I know that, and I know that I hate the gunman and everything he's put us through tonight. I hate him even more for almost making me a murderer.

I almost shot the kid. The knowledge that I could have ended his life hasn't yet left me. My hands still shake. My pulse still pounds. My anger still thrums. My cell phone battery remains at two percent. If that light goes out, we'll be more alone here than we've been so far. The only thing currently keeping the boy's blood from bubbling out is the extra tee that once served as Teddy's change of clothes, now wrapped tight and double-knotted just under the boy's shoulder.

His head now rests in my lap. Aiming the phone light directly on the boy's shoulder, I keep my hand pressed over the hole and cry while Teddy racks his brain for a new idea.

"Can I use your jacket?" he asks.

"Of course. Do you need me to help tear it?"

"No, I'm just going to ball it up and stuff it underneath his shoulder to catch the blood from the other side. Maybe if it slows, it will have time to clot..." He pauses, takes a few deep breaths. I'm not the only one crying anymore. "I can't think of anything else to do. Nothing else..." Panic rings loud in Teddy's voice, guilt deepening the sound.

"Get my jacket, Teddy. You're doing great. This isn't your fault. None of this is your fault."

I repeat those last five words while Teddy snatches the

jacket and tucks it quickly under the boy's back. He cries out in pain, his head shifting a bit in my lap. Placing both hands at his temples, I hold him still. I'm not sure if moving around will hurt him, but keeping him still seems to make sense. I stare at his young face; in the dim light, he appears to be early-teens, spots of acne dotting his forehead with its evidence of youth. To think of what this kid has been through adds another layer of sadness to a day that can't take much more. I don't want him to die. I don't want to die. I don't want Teddy to die. Hurt is taking place beyond this door, and the possibility of it infiltrating these walls terrifies me. My job is to take care of Teddy, but I'm not sure I can protect them both. One women, one gun, three men if that door opens. The odds are stacked against us even before the dice are rolled.

Teddy's shoulder brushes my chest as he dabs at the boy's wounds. "It's my fault. All of it. You don't have to tell me otherwise."

His voice has no inflection, just matter-of-fact resignation. My heart crashes to the floor. There's more defeat in his words than one person can repair. I say nothing because there's nothing to say. Lies scream louder than the truth anyway.

The boy lies still, my hand on his chest. There's a slight up and down movement that relaxes me a bit. I shift to bring my legs out in front of me and lean against the wall. I'm tired. Teddy seems more so. It's coming up on two hours, and I want this nightmare to end. Teddy turns off the phone and settles in next to me. He's holding the jacket in place, I'm holding the shirt. Our hands touch, but it isn't awkward; oddly enough, it's the most familiar thing in my world now, like a stranger's sweater you try on at a rummage sale that instantly feels like it belongs to you. In this room, his touch belongs to me...something I'll miss when we're gone. The one beautiful thing in a big patch of ugly. I place my hand on his. Teddy's fingers lock around mine one at a time and settle on top of the boy's still moving chest. We stay that way, side-by-side in a newly formed ring of three.

"When I was a kid," he whispers, "I wanted to be a doctor. A pediatric surgeon, specifically. My cousin Dillon—the one I was telling you about that wants me to be her maid of honor—lost an older brother before she was born. He was four. Died from leukemia. She's been sad about it her whole life even though she never knew him. Still is from time to time, especially around the anniversary. When we were young, I promised her that I would be a doctor one day so I could save all the little kids in her brother's name." He takes a slow breath. "I meant it, but then music started to become my passion. I was good at it, you know? And eventually, it took over, and the doctor thing left completely. Every once in a while, I wonder if I should have pursued it. I don't think about it often, but I'm thinking about it now. There isn't much worse than knowing your older brother didn't get to live while you did."

There isn't much worse.

He has no way of knowing, but he's just hit a soft spot inside me that hasn't been touched in years. An old familiar swirl of blacks and blues and purples mixed in with familiar sharp red streaks snake through my mind. The red hurts like a bullet, exactly the way it should. His reasons for wanting to become a doctor match my reasons for wanting to protect people.

Half my heart constricts, a throb starting at the core and working its way outward. Everyone experiences heartbreak differently. Mine hits all at once and feels like a thousand bee stings right above my breast bone. The pain is quick, doesn't normally last long, but it's long enough to make catching a breath difficult.

I blink into the darkness, memories hitting so fast that I want to duck and dodge them. But the act would be silly, wouldn't make sense to Teddy, and the boy's head needs to remain still so we can save him. This is what I tell myself, because I need to help somehow. I need to protect someone. I only hope that maybe someday that someone will be me.

I don't tell him he's wrong.

I don't tell him there *is* something worse.

I don't tell him that being the parent of a dead baby is the worst thing of all.

———

Sixteen and pregnant, a child beauty queen suddenly ugly in her actions. A good girl in my church's youth group who turned into a pariah the moment people began to figure it out. My stomach gave it away, or it would have if my boyfriend hadn't brought me up as a prayer need during Wednesday night group without asking my permission. Ah, prayer requests. A wonderful tool when the heart is pure; a powerful weapon when gossip is the real motive. *People needed to know* was his excuse. But what he really needed was their sympathy. He was the pastor's son, and he tossed me into the court of public opinion without bail or a single phone call or even a cup of water. They say opinions are formed in the first four months of pregnancy, but I'm here to tell you they happen overnight when all eyes turn toward you with judgment in them.

The youth pastor asked everyone to keep it quiet.

His wife listed off my options.

I chose to keep the baby, but the baby didn't keep me. She

came early at just under thirty weeks. Born at 2:32am and died at 2:39am. Most of me died the very next minute.

The entire church delivered meals...to my boyfriend's family.

They delivered silence to me.

The next day all communication ceased.

Including his. We broke up while I was in the hospital and I haven't seen him since. Closure is a funny word, one that rarely—if ever—comes to pass. You live with an ache that never goes away. You look down every sidewalk hoping an answer will walk by. I've looked on every block in every city I've visited, but I haven't passed one since.

The next week we found a new church.

The next month we quit going altogether. The critical stares followed me everywhere and only got worse. I had soiled the pastor's son; those were the words of many. Why would we willingly subject ourselves to that sort of treatment? It's a funny question with a poetic answer.

You don't. In fact, you do the worst thing you can: you close off so completely that you can't love or be loved...not by anyone at all. And then you travel so far down that winding road that you can't find a way back, so lost on the pathway that eventually you stop looking altogether. Love is pointless, anyway. It only obliterates your heart into pieces you no longer recognize.

The next year I quit God completely. When you lose a baby—even if you were scared, even if it wasn't planned, even if you slept with your boyfriend only once and would rewind time if given the opportunity, even if initially you didn't really want the baby at all—you lose faith. In humanity, in yourself, in God.

Now, looking at this kid lying on my lap, I feel myself wanting a little of that faith back.

I'm pretty sure God is the only one who can get us out of this.

————

Teddy

Something's changed about Jane. She's quiet, hasn't said a word in minutes, not even when I told her I thought the kid might live. One minute we worked frantically to save him, but when I announced his heartbeat was stronger, his breathing more regular, that he would ultimately be fine as long as this ordeal didn't last into next week, she said nothing. It happened when I mentioned Dillon's brother. I'm not sure what triggered them, but Jane has skeletons moving around in that closet of hers. I know this because they're currently sharing living space with mine.

"Is there anything you want to talk about? Anything on your mind?"

A shuddering sigh comes up through her toes and manages to break my heart. Those skeletons are covered in a heavy layer of dust from years of being dormant. Maybe I shouldn't nudge them awake, but she needs to know I care. Being in this room for this long makes you reassess everything important. If I die today, I need to go on the heels of a conversation that matters.

Jane sits up a little straighter and shakes her head. "No. There's nothing on my mind."

I nudge her knee a little with my own. "Are you sure? It seemed like—"

"Let's talk about something else, okay?"

I nod. I'm no stranger to uncomfortable topics and the desire to avoid them. Jane needs the mood to lighten, so I wander back to a familiar standby. I only hope it will do the trick.

"Kissing on the beach or kissing in the rain?"

"What?" I can picture the frown on her face even though I still haven't seen her face.

"Say it, Jane. It's time for a new round of that game. Now answer the question, or I win."

She sighs. "The rain, of course. I'm not a big fan of the beach."

"Me either. Too hot."

"Exactly." She sighs. Whatever is on her mind, I'm going to have to work harder to pull her out of it and into this game. I'd give anything to hear her smile again. I go again out of turn.

"Paperbacks or E-readers?"

"It's not your turn, but paperbacks. E-readers suck, although one might come in handy right now."

"Are you trying to tell me you're bored with me?"

I hear it, a small smile.

"Not *bored* exactly..." Her tone lightens, and I give myself a mental high-five.

"I'm offended," I say.

"You'll get over it. Bubble gum or breath mints?"

"Gum, obviously."

"Breath mints would probably be a better choice."

"Don't insult my breath."

"Won't happen again. Okay, my turn." I think for a moment. "Puppies or kittens?"

"Both, but specifically Collie puppies and Scottish fold kittens."

"You have a Scottish fold?"

"No, I want a Scottish fold. I fully intend to buy one someday."

I don't tell her I hate cats but that it's the only cat in the entire world I've considered owning. Taylor Swift has a couple of them. I saw them in Nashville once and fell a little bit in love—with the cats, just so we're clear—and I've tossed around the idea since. I also don't tell her I grew up with a male Collie named Joe and have vowed to own another one when life settles down someday. You can travel with a cat in ways impossible with dogs. After the day we've had, I may go ahead and get both. Waiting for someday suddenly feels foolish.

"Oh, I have one," I say. "Cooking shows or Housewife shows?

"You keep going out of turn."

"Rules were meant to be broken, Jane. Now answer the question."

I can practically hear her frown. "What are Housewife shows?"

"Of Beverly Hills, of Orange County, of Atlanta."

"Oh, ew. Cooking shows for sure."

"Same," I say. "I'm a big fan of the Hell's Kitchen dude."

"You don't strike me as the cooking type."

"I'm totally the cooking type. Or I'd like to be someday."

"Before or after becoming a surgeon?"

"Before for sure. I fear my surgeon days are over."

"You shouldn't give up so soon. Not when—"

Her next words get lost, disappearing somewhere between her throat and her tongue.

Time is cruel. It doesn't allow you to prepare ahead or plan the right way to react. It just starts and stops and gives you nothing but a split second to decide whether to ebb or flow with it. Sometimes even that split second isn't long enough.

Not when gunshots rain.

Not when screams reverberate.

Not when bodies slam together.

One second we're talking. The next I'm on top of her, the kid wedged against the wall somewhere beside us. That's the way life goes when it veers off course with no time to analyze the right and wrong of the decisions you make.

I only have a second.

I have to choose, and as one, two, three, four bullets slam through the door and rush past our heads...

I choose Jane.

CHAPTER TEN

Jane

I can't breathe. He's on top of me, and I'm supposed to be on top protecting him, but bullets are flying over us. Moving seems dangerous, and everything feels wet because I'm crying, and I can't breathe because of my lungs. Fear has squeezed them shut, and the water from my eyes is filling them, and I'm drowning. I'm choking. This is it. This is the moment I die, and everything is just so sad because I wasn't done living.

I think of my mom.

I think of my dad.

I think of my baby.

I think of my co-workers.

I think of my—

Right then and there, I stop thinking and just listen to the sound of my heartbeat.

There comes a time in life when the human heart will test its limits. When the beat is so forceful, the speed is so swift, and the pain is so sharp, that one finally relinquishes the false belief that survival is inevitable. The body can shatter quickly. The spirit can shatter even faster. We're all fragile, we just don't know it until circumstances put us at the edge of our breaking point. Maybe this happens once in a lifetime. Maybe a dozen. It's different for everyone, and no pattern is the same. The only thing for certain is that the heart will release an ache that is both beautiful and crushing, soothing and terrifying, hopeful and final. The ache will grow before it lessens, but one thing is certain——once the heart has been pushed to the limits, the ache never completely goes away.

For me, this has happened twice in my life.

The first time with my baby, a part of my life I never talk about.

The second time, now.

Both times involving a man I'd been with only once.

The similarities end there.

I can't decide whether to roll out from under Teddy and do my job, or curl myself inside in the confines of his body. I wrestle with the decision for one...two seconds and decide to stay put. Bullets are still flying, people are still screaming outside this door, and if Teddy wants to shelter me from the danger, then I want to let him. It's been a long time, too long, since I've allowed anyone to take care of me. I became a security guard for that very reason, so no one would ever need to. No one will know I failed my job, because something tells me he won't blow my secret.

"Are you okay?" Teddy whispers as he raises up a fraction of an inch, elbows on either side of my head. I feel his heartbeat keeping time with mine, pounding with a thud thud thud that's as painful as it is fast. When I crack open my eyelids, he's looking right at me, scanning my face for signs of injury. I glance away before he can see that all my wounds are internal.

"I'm alright, but I'm scared. What if he bursts in here? What if he discovers we've been hiding in here the whole time? What if we don't make it, and where, in God's name, are the police?" My voice is pinched, tight. A hundred more questions are perched on my lips, but Teddy silences them with a soft *shhh*.

"That's a lot of what ifs, but there's no sense borrowing trouble. We've managed to make it this far, I have no reason to believe we won't make it to the end. Something's happening out there. I don't think these bullets are coming from just one gun. I think maybe the police finally have him."

"I think you might be right." I cling to that hope; maybe the police finally got the upper hand. Maybe we're only a few minutes from being rescued.

"We'll be okay."

I think he's saying the words for his own benefit as well as mine. He shifts to the side, his hip on the ground beside me, but he keeps his body angled over mine. I'm okay as long as he doesn't move too far. Another gunshot, followed by another. Teddy's head ducks into my neck, and the kid groans, but at least we're all still alive. I fist Teddy's shirt and try to keep breathing.

"Talk to me, Teddy," I hiccup into his chest. "Tell me something that will take my mind off this."

His breath suspends, but his grip on my waist tightens. I know what hesitation feels like; I've lived under its shadow longer than I've lived outside it. Someone shouts from the other room. I hope it's the police; something tells me it is.

"I'm not sure I'll ever be able to get on a stage after this." He speaks in hurried words, for the first time louder than a whisper. "I've been thinking about it the whole time we've been in here. How am I supposed to keep going like nothing happened? As though it's just business as usual? I'm scheduled to be in Chicago tomorrow night. And I'm just expected to sing up there in front of all those people?"

I don't know why a cold shiver travels down my spine, but it does. If we walk out of this room tonight, I'll know to be more alert, how to hide, how to be better prepared and on guard for my next job. But Teddy...he'll still be in the spotlight. A moving target singing solo in front of thousands of strangers. If someone wanted to finish the job, theoretically, they could. His life doesn't accommodate chances to hide. I was lucky to grab him this time.

"Keep singing, Teddy. Don't let this guy affect you that badly, okay?" *Says the girl who quit living her own life over a decade ago.*

"I'm not sure I can do it."

I breathe into his neck, my hands gripping his back. The sensation of warm air on skin grounds me a little as bullets fly outside the door.

"I know you can. Just one thing at a time. First, we have to get out of this room."

"Please don't tell anyone I said that. Reporters would have a field day at my expense." I feel his lip brush my neck. "Keep this between you and me, okay?" His voice is louder, rising with the noise outside.

"This entire night is between you and me. I won't tell. Take a few days off if you need to. Reschedule some shows. No one would blame you. You're human, Teddy. And you've just been—you're still going through—hell. Don't let anyone make you feel bad if you need some time away, okay?" I'm trying to get the words out in case I can't ever speak again. It's everything I wish someone had said to me.

"Time off is not something I get much of nowadays." His thumb traces a figure eight at my waist. Noise is everywhere, but for now, our little space is sheltered.

"You're the boss, though. Take it anyway if you need it. Other people can wait."

He huffs. "No one who works for me has ever told me to take time off. It's all go go go in this business."

"Then maybe you need to hire different people. It isn't your job to entertain everyone all the time. Maybe you ought to think about entertaining yourself for a bit."

Bold words, but I mean them. Who's taking care of Teddy? And who would discourage a few days off after an ordeal like this? I'd like to find the person who might try and give him a piece of my mind. No one should rule your life other than yourself and God. Not deadbeat teenage boyfriends or judgmental church-goers, neither of which matter anymore. Why am I just now seeing this?

"Promise me you'll take care of yourself first," I say. I'm no longer sure if I'm speaking to Teddy or to my sixteen-year-old self.

He doesn't have time to answer. Something crashes against the door. Teddy buries his head as my panic level rises. It's hard to focus on the here, on the now when the future seems so thoroughly bleak. My fingers dig into his back, his forehead presses into mine.

"Your turn. Tell me something good," he says.

I don't have anything good to share, but I want to tell him the words I've never told anyone else. I want to tell him about all the pent-up feelings I've carried around in my bruised and battered heart all these years. It's such a shame to die with your private sins...with the realization that in a short span of a life, no one ever really knew you at all.

"I had a baby when I was sixteen. I didn't want her at first, but in the end, I did. She was stillborn, and I've always thought it was God's way of punishing me. She would be nine now..."

That's it. My secret leaked out before I could stop it, but that's as much as I can say. Out of habit or stubbornness or simply the same familiar sadness that has always driven me forward, I turn my head to the side. Shame has a way of pulling you under, even if you try to look it in the eye a time or two.

I can't see him, but I can feel his compassion like he's pouring it over me.

"I'm sorry, Jane. He doesn't punish people like that, but thank you for telling me."

Maybe Teddy's right. Maybe He doesn't.

"Can you—"

"I won't tell a soul."

The words hold between us for several seconds.

Then men shout. Objects break. Bullets explode. The world spins outside, but in our little corner, Teddy touches his lips to mine as we listen and block out and try to forget everything together.

None of it makes sense, but all of it does.

I've heard about acquaintances kissing each other during what might be the last moments of their lives. I've always thought the idea was crazy. Impulsive. Foolish.

I still do.

And I don't.

I kiss him back and pray I'll somehow survive this.

———

Teddy

I kissed her even though I shouldn't have.

It only lasted a second before she turned away, but it was long enough.

I won't forget it.

Maybe not ever.

I hold onto her even though letting go is going to hurt.

All hell is breaking loose around us.

Deep down...so is my heart.

I bury my head in her shoulder and pray that both stop soon.

CHAPTER ELEVEN

Jane

It happens so fast I'm not sure if it's real or an illusion. The quiet never returns. The seclusion is a thing of the past. When a fusion of noise hits your ears at full volume after hours and hours of whispered silence, it's especially cruel.

A relief. But still cruel in the rude delivery.

The sound of Jane's walkie blasts though the closet.

"Jane, stay there. They got him. I'll be there to get you both in a few." It's Andy again. She presses the button to respond.

"Okay, but we're under the walkway. Not the main stage."

Silence greets us. So much silence. Followed by an "Oh, dear God."

Jane sets the walkie down. There isn't much to say to that.

Next comes ripping.

Tearing.

Crying.

So much crying.

People start running.

Footsteps pass by the door.

I slide out from underneath Teddy and lunge for my gun, shoving Teddy behind me just in case this isn't over. Between us, there's so much relief I can touch it, smell it, taste it like a sheet of rusty metal at the back of my throat. Teddy links his hand in mine, and as much as I want out, I know I'll miss this one thing the most.

The overhead light flickers on, a shock to the system and the eyes. One hand flies to my eyes, shielding them from what feels like a hundred razorblades pricking at my vision. Darkness does not like to be so rudely interrupted.

"Son of a—" Teddy says out loud before stopping himself. I suck in a breath at hearing his full voice for the first time in here, partly because I'm still afraid we'll get caught, but mostly because it's so perfectly husky and rich. I have nothing to worry about; it's time to be found. It's the reaction my heart just had that could be the real issue. Teddy is bent at the waist, pinching his forehead with a thumb and finger. "A little warning might have been nice."

"No kidding. I feel like someone is stabbing my eyes."

I blink rapidly at the kid lying in a heap in the corner where we left him, both hands folded across his stomach. He looks better than I thought he might, his chest still rises and falls in steady intervals. Teddy lets go of my hand long enough to check the boy's pulse. Satisfied, he reaches for my hand again and finally looks up.

His eyes go wide when they lock on mine, and everything stills. I frown in a question, then grow self-conscious when I remember this is the first time he's seeing me. I squirm under his scrutiny, uncomfortable with his direct appraising gaze.

Jane, hold your head up.

Jane, stand up straight.

Jane, don't you want people to think you're pretty?

Jane, why can't you act like a proper lady just once?

The disappointment is there like a friend I've known

forever.

———

Teddy

I can't move.

Can't breathe.

The shock of the light, the shock of the room, the shock of seeing her like this is too much.

Chaos reigns on the other side of this door, the only thing currently outranking the chaos inside my head and heart.

I had a thousand visions of Jane during our time in this room, but none of them matched reality.

She's tall, nearly as tall as me.

She's beautiful.

Achingly, heartbreakingly so.

A green-eyed, heroic blonde bombshell vision I won't ever forget.

In only a handful of minutes, I'll have to.

I swallow my reaction. My hammering pulse. My feelings...and speak.

"You ready for this?"

She gives a little shake of her head, and my hand involuntarily squeezes around hers. Mine. Hers. For one more second, we own each other. Until we don't.

"I guess we have to be," she says.

No truer words were ever spoken.

———

Jane

Andy opens the door, a policeman on his heels.

"You guys okay?" Andy asks. The policeman walks around us and into the room.

I nod once, twice. Still clutching Teddy's hand, planning to never let go.

"We are, but he needs help." I indicate the kid still lying on the floor, still blessedly asleep. I checked his breathing a few seconds ago to make sure it still existed. It did, thank God. A paramedic is called and enters the room before we take a step. It's all so clinical, professional. Every team has a protocol and every person is following it. Except me. I'm just trying to stay upright.

After years of hiding in here, we slowly, cautiously, allow ourselves to be led back the way we came.

Within two heartbeats, I wish to God we hadn't.

Nothing could prepare me for this. I've been sucker-punched, taken down at the knees, force-fed poison, and I can't spit it out.

I remember a gleaming floor and the lingering smell of disinfectant. I remember the scent of beer and the smiling face of a teenage boy. I remember newly purchased t-shirts and tiny waving glow sticks.

The arena looks nothing like the place I remember from seven hours ago.

The catwalk stage is bent on one side; misshapen cups of soda are scattered everywhere. Discarded pieces of clothing are lying all over—jackets, ties, a random pair of socks, a woman's hair tie. Glass drapes the floor in a thick dusting of uncut diamonds—sparkling jewels that gash, tear, wound, leave scars. Blood stains the floors in swirls and smears. His blood. Her blood. In the five seconds, we've stood here, I've counted three bodies.

I want to vomit.

I'm going to vomit.

I lunge for an empty popcorn bucket, and Teddy holds my hair back while I release everything I haven't eaten in the past twelve hours. The plan was to grab dinner after the show.

The show's over now, but the thought of food repulses me. Somehow I manage to empty my stomach of its meager contents. When I'm finished, I stand and wipe my mouth with the back of my hand. I'm certain the horror on my face matches the dismay I see on Teddy's.

The gunman was after Teddy specifically.

This was his concert.

This was his night.

People paid for a chance to see him.

It cost them more than money.

This isn't fair. Life isn't fair. None of us did anything to deserve this kind of cruelty.

Teddy reaches for me, hooks his arm around my neck, and brings my face to his chest.

"Don't look, Jane. Keep your head down."

"I have to look at it. I have to make sure they're okay, that you're okay."

The sob that catches in his throat nearly unravels me, but this isn't the time for weakness. I make eye contact with a few battered people staring in our direction; most tending to wounds both visible and invisible on themselves, on their neighbors, on their loved ones. Pain is everywhere. Fear is everywhere. Sadness is everywhere.

Police are everywhere. One of them points to us. Andy stands next to him.

"You both need to sit there and wait until we come back."

It's an order. He means business. They're taking precautions with Teddy and won't allow disobedience. I don't have the strength to protest anyway.

Exhausted and overwhelmed with grief and unbelief, I drop into a chair, one hand firmly locked around my gun and the other still clutching Teddy's hand. My eyes leak in rivers, my stomach growls with hunger, but I'm numb in every other way that matters. I've trained for this, but in all my months of preparing to be a bodyguard, the reality doesn't come close. How can someone point and shoot so callously at people? Everyone here is someone's child, and would blend in with the huddle on a daily walk down the street. The loss of life and innocence is staggering.

Teddy reaches for my hand and brings it to his face. My hand is cold, his lips are not. "Are you going to be okay?"

I won't. I never will be again. But sometimes the mouth speaks lies even while the mind gets busy burying the truth. So I nod. Just once. Once doesn't seem quite as fake as three.

"I'll be okay. Will you? That's the important part."

I feel his hesitation in the slow way he exhales. "My life is no more important than anyone else's. But yes, eventually. Probably."

I know we're both lying. If someone presented us with a lie detector test, our result would be a series of jagged lines and accelerated pulses and flashing red lights.

But we sit side-by-side, waiting for our turn to speak while I still clutch my gun, something I'll continue to do until I'm certain this ordeal is over. I'll answer all the questions, I'll submit to all the probing, I'll agree to the calls for counseling, I'll continue on to the next job as though this one never happened.

But the truth...

The real way I'm feeling...

I'll keep most of that to myself.

———

Teddy

Two hours later, I'm as unprepared for the night air outside as I was for the lights in the closet. It's jarring and surreal, like freedom after the shackles are off. I don't know what to do with the sensation. I don't know what happens now. A police officer escorted us backstage so I could grab my phone and change my shirt. I checked my messages to see nearly a hundred texts from friends and family, and I've downed a beer I swiped from the green room. I offered one to Jane, but she turned it down. I'm once again clutching her hand even though my own bodyguards are with me now, and I'm almost certain it's time to let go of her. I don't, not yet. Some habits take time to break, even the new ones.

She spent her night taking care of me, putting her life on the line for mine. I feel like I owe her...something. My time, if nothing else. As long as we're in this parking lot, there's still some left.

"This way," the cop says, leading me off to the side. I drag Jane with me, and she doesn't protest. If she has a boss to check in with, she doesn't make an effort. So far, she's kept conversations to her partner and me, otherwise staying silent. There's a lot going on in Jane's head, but none of it has made its way out. I keep hold of her hand in case a few words climb to the surface.

Blue lights from police cars light up the night sky, and people mill through the parking lot in singles and groups alike. Crying victims sit with blankets over their shoulders as ambulances are loaded with the most precarious individuals— some laid out with oxygen masks covering their faces, others stretched flat and lying still, sheets draped across their heads. Like the rest of the country, I've seen this on the news a hundred times before. Watching devastation and living it aren't in the same realm. I look away, not yet willing to let reality grab hold of my insides just yet. I'm at the edge of a cesspool of emotion, but I'm not ready to break. I'll do that later when I'm home and alone.

It's dark and November, but I've forgotten how cold it is outside. Even though I've changed, my back is still sticky with perspiration from the sweltering closet. Or maybe from

nerves. Sweat crystallizes down my spine in the chilly air, and
I shiver. Normally, after a concert I'm on edge and high-
strung from left-over energy. Now I'm only on-edge. Seven
hours might be just another partial rotation on the Earth's
axis, but in those few hours, everything changed.

All I can think of is Jane. In an unfair handful of minutes,
I have to tell her goodbye.

This is what I'm thinking about when I hear it—the call
of my name by a few very familiar voices. A few days ago, the
voices made me feel at home. Tonight, I feel both unease and
relief. I turn and let go of Jane's hand. Goodbye is here,
whether I like it or not.

Before I look up, a female form rushes into my arms,
followed by two men and another woman on the outskirts of
the group.

"Thank God you're okay," my cousin Dillon says, burying
her face into my chest. She's crying and shaking. My roommate Liam gives her a minute before blessedly pulling her off
me. Dillon is my best friend, but she can sometimes smother.
Right now, I just need a second.

"Give him some room, Dillon. You're going to crush him."
Liam says.

She steps back and looks up at me. "I was so worried. We
flew here on the first flight out. It was terrifying, Teddy. No
one would tell us what was happening, and the news kept
getting everything wrong. The media is a joke."

"I've been telling you that for years," I say to the group.
"But none of you ever listen."

Dillon, Liam, Chad, and his girlfriend Riley laugh a little.
The first time I saw Riley, her hair was pink, the second time
it was brown, and now it's fringed in blue. For as conservative
and boring Chad almost always is, his girlfriend is cool.

"I believe you now. If anything had happened to you..."

"It didn't." I kiss Dillon on the forehead and loop my arm

over her shoulder. "You still have a maid of honor, but I'm still not wearing a dress."

Liam laughs. "She asked you already, did she?"

I shoot him a look. "Right before I went onstage." I rub the top of her head with my knuckles. "Worst timing ever, by the way."

"Well, I needed to know. So I can decide on the dress color."

Liam smiles, but he turns serious when he looks at me. "You okay?"

I nod. The levity is nice, but my insides are still mangled and sick. I remember Jane then and turn to find her behind me. Reluctance paints her countenance, but I reach for her hand and pull her forward into our group.

"This one dragged me into a closet under the stage and saved my life. She was hired by the venue to keep the place secure tonight, but she wound up being my temporary body-guard. Without her..." My voice cracks with emotion. Both Liam and Chad catch it and check me with a look.

Her, huh? Their eyes communicate meaning in nearly the same way; as brothers, it isn't surprising. Chad's smile is so faint that you wouldn't notice if you didn't know what to look for. I know, and I narrow my gaze.

No, not her. Probably. Shut up.

Chad's hand comes out to shake Jane's. "Thank you for taking care of him. He can be a bit of a diva, but we couldn't live without him." A chorus of murmured thank yous follow.

"He wasn't too bad," Jane says shyly. "A little demanding at times, but not awful." She smiles, a faint blush creeping up her neck. I'm struck once again by her looks, beautiful to match the personality I pieced together in the dark. She looks pointedly at Dillon. "But, I'm thinking red."

Three sets of eyes frown at her, four if you count mine. Only Dillon laughs. She gets the comment immediately.

"Red! That's perfect. And it gives me an idea..."

I'm still lost...until I'm not. Give me a break. "I am not wearing a red dress," I protest, looping my other arm around Jane. "And no one asked you anyway." Both women laugh like they've been best friends for years, and I resent it and like it at the same time. I'm not ready to share her yet. Jane's mine, even if she isn't.

The thought startles me in its directness. *Jane's mine?*

"Jane?"

A voice I don't recognize calls from behind us. I'm looking at her when the smile drops off her face, and I turn to see who's calling for her. A man. My age, maybe a bit older. Red hair. Stubble lining his chin. Nice looking enough, but I've never met him before. It takes a minute, but when Jane ducks from under my arm and takes a step away, I know.

"Ben," she says, moving close enough to let him pull her into a hug.

She never mentioned a Ben.

When he kisses her, everything sinks. She can't be mine when she so clearly belongs to someone else, even if she never thought to bring him up. No wonder her head turned during that kiss. It confused me then, but suddenly it makes sense. Ben. The fourth person in the room, even if I didn't know he existed.

I'm gawking before I realize everyone notices. Conscious of the stares of way too many people aimed at me, I clear my throat and step forward, extending my hand. I'm casual, that's me. I could not care less.

"Ben, I've heard all about you." A lie that surprises Jane, judging by the look in her eyes. He tucks Jane underneath his arm—the guy's a head taller than me, which I don't appreciate—and she plasters on what looks like an insincere smile. I've only seen her real smile twice, so I can't be completely sure.

"Yes, he's heard stories. You run out of things to talk about when you're locked up together."

You don't, but no one else needs to know that.

"Wow, how lucky were you that you got to be the one to save Teddy Hayes. It's already all over the news."

My neck snaps back before I can stop it. Is he kidding? "I wouldn't call it luck, but I am thankful she was there."

"Not much feels lucky when there's a gunman in the room," Jane agrees.

Ben stammers a bit on the backtrack. "I just meant I'm glad you got to save him. Everyone's talking about my cool girlfriend."

I don't point out that he should be talking about her.

"She is pretty cool," I agree, and decide to leave it at that.

I glance at Jane, but she's looking everywhere but at me. I catch her gaze on a sweep-by and see a raincloud—dark and stormy, with a little moisture behind the folds. She stares at me, tilts her head in question, then turns her gaze toward her boyfriend, who's moved on to complimenting me on my fabulous career, voice, and latest album. It's entirely possible I'm having a visceral reaction to the guy because I'm jealous. But sue me, I don't like him. I also have no idea what to say until Jane's voice cuts into his monologue.

"We should probably let Teddy get back to his friends, Ben. Besides, I'm tired and need to talk to the police before I can leave."

"Alright, I'll come with you. But give them the short and sweet version so we can get out of here." He still hasn't asked about her state of mind, so I make it my business to ask her myself.

"You sure you're okay, Jane? I can arrange a driver to get you home, order you some food, whatever you want."

She smiles, but it's small. Nothing like the smile she gave when laughing with Dillon about red dresses. Megawatt and powerful then, now it's reminiscent of the closet: dim and hard to see, even if you search for it.

"I'm fine." She takes a deliberate step back and hugs her arms to her chest. "A little shaken up, but fine. I don't think I could eat anything now anyway." She makes a show of messing with her jacket, her holster, her belt, but her eyes keep flicking my direction when she thinks I'm not looking. I haven't stopped, so I catch every one.

With Jane, I'm catching everything.

"I could eat something," Ben says, ripping me from my thoughts. "And a ride would be great. I took a cab to get here."

It's all I can do to stop an eye roll. How come he gets to go with her while I stay here? Jealousy is ugly, and it plays guitar.

"Yeah, okay." I raise a finger to summon Jack, our driver.

"Yeah, boss?"

"When they're ready, could you run these two wherever they need to go? And take them somewhere to get food? I'll still be here for quite a while, so however long it takes is fine."

"Teddy, please don't—"

I cut Jane off after three words. "It's the least I can do. And here." I pull my wallet from my back pocket and slip out a fifty, nonchalantly folding it around a business card that contains my cell phone number, email, and home address. Nothing subtle about it, but I'm suddenly desperate for a way to get in touch with her, even if it means being reliant on her to make the first move.

"I'm not taking your money," she says.

"Don't fight me on this," I say back. "You might have been in charge in the closet, but I'm in charge out here."

Dillon laughs once, but covers it with a cough. She stops when I shoot her a look.

"I wouldn't test him if I were you," she sings.

"Fine," Jane reluctantly agrees, flashing an embarrassed but beautiful smile when she meets my eyes. She takes the money. A little thrill runs through me when she spots the card and tucks it into her back pocket, though the move almost certainly means nothing.

"You're welcome." I take a deep breath. It's the moment of truth. "Alright, you'll call me if you need anything?"

She nods, then hesitates. Goodbyes are hard under normal circumstances, but this one is different. Threads between Jane and I were woven and tangled inside that closet, and I have no idea how to undo the knots. It's almost painful, like I'm letting go of half my insides, breaking free from a bond glued tight and unrelenting. My breath catches, and at the same time, my heart constricts. I'm awkward and hesitant, wanting to stake my claim while being unable to. Her boyfriend is watching, and any claim is imaginary.

I pull her into a hug that surprises us both, hearing it on her intake of breath. "Take care, Jane," I whisper into her ear, hoping she can hear the emotion around it. If it wasn't for her, I might not be alive. And that's the sobering truth of the situation. I owe her everything, and I'm sending her off with fifty bucks, a phone number, and a guy who still hasn't asked how she's doing.

She nods and I let go, watching as she links her hand through his, and they walk off together. It aches...my chest. Another side-effect of a terribly effed-up night.

"Oh no," Liam says next to me. I snap out of my pity party and glance at him.

"What?"

"Someone's got it bad. What, my friend, are we going to do about this?"

I want to tell him to shut up, but I don't.

How do you argue with someone who knows what he's talking about?

CHAPTER TWELVE

Jane

In four days, I've gone from a girl who slept at least nine hours a night, lest the inner black-winged demons reveal themselves the next morning, to a compulsive insomniac. I haven't slept since the arena. Exhaustion is continuously at the forefront of my brain, at the heavy joints in my limbs, but I can't make myself settle down long enough to drift into anything more than a light nap that lasts no more than fifteen minutes a stretch.

I lay down, I think of Teddy.

I get up, I think of Teddy.

I shower, I think of Teddy.

I have a boyfriend.

A boyfriend who has left me three texts in the past five minutes.

Do these thoughts make me a cheater?

Why didn't I tell Teddy about him in the closet?

I know why. Because I never thought of Ben. In what could have been my last moments on earth, I didn't give him a thought. Isn't that when you're supposed to quickly reflect on everything important in life?

I barely dwell on that revelation, because when I reach for coffee...I'm back to thinking of Teddy.

I think of Teddy until I remember the bodies inside the arena. Until I remember the kid in the closet, who did, in fact, make it, though his eyesight is missing on one side. He wasn't the only one to walk away changed.

One woman lost her leg.

Six people remain in intensive care, clinging to life through feeding tubes and heart monitors.

One man is brain-dead, but his daughter refuses to let him go.

Five people were killed, two of them children. I'll never get the image of the aftermath out of my mind, no matter how long I live.

The gunman was a forty-nine-year-old ex-college professor of physics who thought shooting up a concert would be, "different." His word, delivered casually with a shrug. He had no history of violence, no past trouble at the school. *Norman wouldn't hurt a fly.* It's always the nice quiet ones, isn't it? He's currently being held in the state prison, awaiting a trial date. His female lawyer is all over the news screaming for prisoner's rights and the fair treatment of the mentally ill. To be clear, there's no indication of mental illness in his past. So to her claims, I say he should have the same rights as the rest of us who never asked for any of this.

Maybe that's cruel of me, but it's only been four days.

Give me a year, and maybe I'll feel differently.

The good news is, except for one jerk on social media whose entire feed is dedicated to taking celebrities down, no one is blaming Teddy. Except, I suspect, Teddy himself. He canceled a concert in Chicago three nights ago and isn't expected to appear in Denver tonight. The "flu" was the official statement given this time. I'm fairly certain the only thing currently sick about Teddy is his mind. My own mind is a shredded mess. It's witnessed too much in the last few days; things it may never heal from completely.

Death is a hard thing to shoulder—a grandparent's death, a coworker's death, the idea of my own death. But a child's? Nothing prepares you for the grim finality of witnessing the end of a life that barely got a chance to start, even if you're technically trained for it.

Even if you've absolutely seen it.

The clock beside my bed won't stop playing some cheesy eighties song, so I slap it in frustration and sit up, rubbing my eyes. Stupid alarm and its knack for terrible timing. I have a work meeting in an hour and zero desire to go. Another briefing, another timeline, another day spent accounting for every second spent in that closet because the police want answers and lawyers are working to build a case. I briefly consider claiming the flu as well, but I can't afford to take more time off. I read the texts from Ben; three successive texts asking for favors.

Hey, I forgot to pick up the dry cleaning. Can you do that before you come into work? The store opens at 8:00.

Great. It's seven already. That doesn't give me much time.

Hey, remember it's Wednesday. The guys are coming to my place to watch the game tonight.

Good. I could use a night to myself.

Hey, can you grab some coffee on your way in? I need another cup. You wouldn't believe the day I've had.

I could use four, but suddenly I have lots of errands.

I throw back the covers with a growl and walk to the bathroom, locking the door behind me, a new habit I've developed in the last few days. A girl can never be too safe. I have one foot inside the shower when I hear the knock at the door, which just figures because why should life be easy?

I reach for a towel and wrap it around me when I hear the rattle of a key, the turn of a doorknob. My heartbeat accelerates a bit before it hits me; I don't have to step outside this bathroom to know who just walked in. She's called every hour of every day for four days, but of course, she chooses now to finally show up. I have errands to run. I have a job to get to. I have jittery co-workers to deal with. I have post-traumatic stress anxiety, I think. The list of grievances keep piling up.

"Allison Jane, what do you think you're doing?" Only my mother would call me this. Only my mother would dare.

"I'm trying not to be naked when you walk in here, Mom." Hearing footsteps quickly approaching, I tuck the towel into itself and crack the door open. My mother's eyes meet me in the narrow space right before she bursts all the way into the room. I make a growling noise that doesn't deter her in the slightest. "Do you mind? Some of us like to be fully clothed when guests show up."

"I'm not a guest."

She brushes past me to check her teeth in the bathroom mirror. I lean against the counter and curse the glass for not yet fogging over.

"What are you doing here so early?"

Satisfied, she straightens. "The counseling center called. You didn't show up yesterday."

I cross my arms over my chest and look at the floor. "Why did they call you? They have no right to just—"

"I'm paying the bill, so of course they have a right. More importantly, *I* have a right to know if my daughter is shrugging off her mental health at a time like this. Do you know how high your odds are of slipping into depression after a trauma like you've been through? Do you know that suicide risks increase after being held at gunpoint? After being forced against your will to..."

"Mom, you do know it's my job, right?"

She sighs, long and loud, the way mothers have perfected over centuries of helicopter parenting. I wonder if Jesus rolled his eyes when his mother sighed. Hey Mary, did you know that you sometimes drove the Savior of the world absolutely bonkers? Now there's a line in the Christmas song no one ever sings.

"It's your job to protect people, but not at your own peril."

And this is where I tune her out, because that is the exact definition of my job. And of course, I know the odds. She's recited them to me word for word no less than one hundred times since I walked out of that arena. I'm so sick of hearing about the odds that part of me would like to shut myself back inside that closet and spend the next twenty-four hours in darkness and solitude.

What's worse, my mother is a yoga instructor at the local gym. With about ten loyal clients. All of her supposed knowledge? She got it from Wikipedia. What's worse than that? I should have known agreeing to let her pay for my sessions would come with thick black drawstrings attached to the arrangement. My mother never does anything just because.

"Are you even listening to me?" She does that thing. That mom thing where one eyebrow raises slowly like a knife, just before it cuts you down the middle.

"I heard every word," I lie. "I'll go today. If they call you back, tell them I'll be there at four." I might as well be agreeing to have all my teeth pulled, that's how enthusiastic I sound.

She gives a single nod. "That's what I like to hear." She eyes the towel, my dirty hair, my make-up free face. "Don't you need to be at work?"

I do. But this is only a cursory question for my mother; she doesn't give me a chance to respond.

"Jane, get in the shower." She sighs and walks out of the bathroom, calling behind herself. "You'd never get anywhere on time if I didn't show up to see to it."

I bite my lip. Drop the towel. Wait, stark naked, for the pause at the kitchen counter as she rifles through my mail. The suction of the refrigerator as she helps herself to a water bottle. The squeak of the front door as she opens it. The turn of the lock as she leaves.

And after I hear those things?

The four-letter words start flying.

———

Teddy

"You can't have her."

My menacing words are a command, but they don't elicit the reaction I expect. The man laughs, just laughs, while I stare him down onstage. Spotlights blind me, but I can see his face clearly. He has the oddest beard, shaved close at the sides, long and pointed at the front, three inches...four inches in length, and I can't stop staring at it. I want to reach out and pull it off, but I can't move my arms. They're weighted, numb like I've slept on them all night. I drop the microphone I'm holding and watch it roll across the floor. But I don't care about it; Jane is behind me, and this man is trying to take her.

"Did you hear me?" I say again. "I said you can't have her."

The man just grins like a man who shares secrets with the devil.

Raises a gun.

And shoots Jane in the head.

The bullet exits and whizzes right over my left shoulder.

I open my mouth to scream, but nothing comes out. I'm

underground. I have no voice. My body starts shaking. Shaking and shaking and shaking while my mouth fills with cement. This is how I die, alongside Jane, too powerless to save either one of us while the crowd watches it all unfold. I try again to cry out, but my voice no longer works.

"Teddy! Stop punching me! Stop punching me and wake up!"

I open my eyes and jerk upright. I'm in bed. I'm in my bed. This is my bedroom. There is no man, no gun, no cement.

No dead Jane.

I fall back and blink up at the ceiling as pain and prickling work their magic to return my arms to normal. I must have slept on them all night again. That's the weirdest thing about the last four days. I used to be an insomniac who tossed and turned and thought a good night's sleep consisted of three straight hours. Now I sleep all night in an unmoving position, my subconscious plagued with so many flashbacks and wild scenarios that I feel like I've run a marathon each morning when I finally wake up.

I'm drenched in sweat, and my heart clocks a thousand beats a minute. The marathon isn't just a metaphor.

"When did you get here?" I blink up at Dillon and squeeze my eyes shut to clear them. "And what time is it?"

"I got here a few minutes ago, and it's eight o'clock. Liam's in the shower, getting ready to help me register for wedding gifts. I could hear you hollering when I walked in the front door. You're still having nightmares?"

"I'm still having nightmares." I tunnel my fingers through my hair and look at her, working up what I hope passes for an unaffected smile. "They'll stop soon, don't worry." Dillon may be my cousin and best friend, but half the time, she's also my mother. It's an odd dynamic that works for us, even though everyone outside our family thinks it's weird.

Her expression is lined with worry. It's a look I'm getting used to from her...one I'll learn to live with. I'm tired of the questions, and I'll do anything to keep her concern at bay. Even lie straight to her face. I don't think they'll stop anytime soon. It's the reason I can't bring myself to get back onstage.

She sighs and pulls at a loose thread on my comforter. "Your manager wants you to go to counseling today. I'm not sure he's right, but I do know you're not going to get back to normal if you keep pushing it all down. You need to talk to someone about these dreams, even if it's just Chad or Liam."

"Is my manager calling you?"

"Only when he can't get ahold of you. He said he's been trying since yesterday morning, and you won't answer."

"That's because I don't want to talk. What I want is to be left alone for a few days."

"He says it's been four days since the incident, Teddy. I don't know what to tell him."

It's been four days. I saw dead people lying prone on the floor and took sub-par care of a young kid who only has one functioning eye because I missed that particular wound in the dark when I was focusing on his shoulder, and all of this happened at *my* concert, which means all the blame lies with me...but it's been four days. Nothing prepares you for that kind of disaster. And the worst part? I'm fully aware it could happen again inside any random arena.

How am I supposed to risk that again?

"Do you think I should go?" Dillon is a counselor. Her expert opinion is the one I'll follow. If she tells me no, my manager can screw himself, at least for the next few days.

She looks at me, her shoulders sagging with weighted concern. "Right now? No. I think you should take a few days to process things by yourself. It will be hard to talk to someone before you know how you really feel about it. But later? Say, next week? Yes. You should go at that point. I know you. You'll close off and push down, and that kind of reaction isn't good for anyone."

"You don't know me *that* well," I mumble.

"We swapped pacifiers in the crib, dude. And we took a blood oath when we were seven. I know you better than anyone. But if I ever find out you told Mrs. Peterman about the baby chick I stole out of her henhouse..."

The memory makes me smile. "Never. Blood's blood, except I still think you should've let me cook him when he got older."

"Henry? He was my pet, and that's just cruel." She shoves me on the side. "Wait a few days on counseling, but then go. At least once, so Mike will stop calling to ask."

I turn her words over in my mind, then nod. "I'll go next week and talk to him about the dreams." I'll do whatever as long as the worry in her eyes will go away. "But right now, you need to grab your lazy-butt fiancé and go pick out a toaster."

She laughs and reaches for her purse, then slides it over her shoulder. "I think he's still in the shower."

"That's because he takes the longest showers in the history of mankind. Uses all the hot water, too. Want me to kick him out?"

"No, I'll yell at him to hurry." Dillon looks down at me, her light smile fading into a weighted frown. "Get some rest, okay? I'm worried about you."

I reach for her hand and give it a gentle shake. "I know you are. I'll try."

"What about your concert?"

I sigh. "I already canceled it."

She doesn't respond, which is definitely a response.

"I'm not ready, Dillon. Eventually, I will be, but not yet."

She sighs. "I don't blame you. Take some time off and rest. Maybe you'll feel better about things next week. Maybe by Flagstaff, especially since you've been so excited about it."

"Maybe." It's the closest I can bring myself to agree with her. I smile up at her to make my one-word lie more believable.

But when she walks out, the smile slips.

Flagstaff. I don't want to perform in Flagstaff or Denver or anywhere else for that matter. It won't make me feel better. How can it when all I can visualize is that kid slowly losing his sight in the closet? What could possibly make me feel better about that?

The thought of being onstage...putting all those people in danger...putting myself in danger.

I know I promised, but some promises are made to be broken.

CHAPTER THIRTEEN

Jane

"Jane, your hand is shaking. Do you want to take a break?"

I startle, then feel my false bravado slide away at the look on Andy's face. He's worried, his freckles darkening the way they sometimes do when he's sleep-deprived and anxious. He was in the arena as well, and he's having nearly as much trouble as I am at night, so much so that his wife has taken to sleeping in the guest bedroom for now. All his tossing and turning apparently freaked her out; though, in my opinion, she's working the victim card a bit much. I don't like people who make things about themselves when they weren't involved. Sweet Andy hasn't said a word, making him the far better man than I would be in that situation.

"Ah, she's doing okay," Ben answers for me. "The faster she gets her routine back, the faster she can put this behind her." He aims and shoots a perfect bullseye. He's trying to help, trying to put a positive spin on my state of mind. I know he is. But he's wrong.

Andy cuts a glance in Ben's direction. "I kinda doubt she'll be able to fully put it behind her. I won't be able to." He turns to me. "But right now, I'm worried about your hands. They're all over the place."

I look at my hands and see the evidence of his claim; they are shaking badly. So badly that I haven't come close to hitting the target. Worse, I don't even recall shooting the gun at all, a definite danger considering my profession. Daydreaming on the job won't get me promoted. Or trusted.

"I think I need a break." I study the target hanging on the wall a hundred feet in front of me and set down the gun, feeling nothing but numbness. My heart isn't here, and neither is my mind. Truthfully, I'm not sure they ever have been.

I fought hard to move up the ranks as an officer, even harder to work a big arena. After I lost my daughter, after I lost my boyfriend, after I lost my innocence—let's just call it what it was—the need to be in control was a strong one. You can only lose so much before you decide to start taking things back. It seemed the best route to self-defense was to become an expert in it. One bullet. Two. Ten thousand. Shooting at the memories, shooting at the failures, shooting at the losses, shooting my demons one by one, hoping they might one day be obliterated. Turns out, there's a wrong way to confront your problems. You can fight them, defend them, grow physically stronger to combat them, even imagine them as paper targets that you fill with holes day after day after day.

But until you talk about them and face them and call them out for what they are, they'll just grow in size and shape. While I was actively busy not looking, my problems spent the past decade lifting weights until they're now stronger than me. I didn't realize how strong, until I shared them with Teddy inside the confines of that closet and broke down from the confession.

I'd never shared that story with anyone until I shared it

with him. Not even with Ben. Even now, I don't want to talk about it.

"Alright, I need coffee," Andy says, slipping off his goggles. I follow suit, jumping when Ben shoots twice without breaking stride. My pulse ricochets to my throat, making it hard to breathe. It's one thing to shoot your own gun. Now, what once sounded like power sounds like fear of the worst kind, especially when someone else is pulling the trigger. "Let's take a fifteen-minute break, and then we'll get back to it."

"I could use some coffee, too. All this shooting is making me nervous."

I feel his side-eye without turning my head to look at him. "You're having trouble moving on, aren't you?"

"Says the man who's currently sleeping solo."

"I know. Apparently, I yelled in my sleep last night. So loud, my wife heard it from across the house."

"Understandable. I'm still sleeping with the light on when I even sleep at all."

We both laugh, but as it fades away, my insides slowly grow numb again. Is there a point to any of this? Life is short, too short. It could end tomorrow, and all I can think is...is this the way I want to live mine? Is this how I want to spend my time? And why can't I stop thinking about Teddy? Even now, as my boyfriend practices target shooting twenty paces away, I miss Teddy. I miss him, but I can't call him, even if he did give me that card. It's inappropriate, which means the only person who can relate to the way I'm feeling is either married, or a thousand miles away and off-limits completely.

We reach the coffee cart, and Andy hands me a cup. Here I am surrounded by co-workers, doing what only last week I considered to be a favorite part of the job. But as the sound of gunshots explodes in the background, gray loneliness settles around me. Familiar tears prick behind my eyes, and I sniff to chase them away. Maybe my mother was right. Maybe I won't skip that counseling appointment after all.

————

Teddy

Counseling is for the weak, even if Dillon is the one who recommended this particular one.

I'm embarrassed, and more than a little angry at his line of questioning, but I can't think of a good lie to redirect his scrutiny. I glance at my arm and resist the urge to cover up the scar. I have nothing to be ashamed of, and I'm certainly not going to let him think he's beaten me. I've been here all of five minutes; if he is going to start with this crap, I'll finish with it. I put this behind me in middle school; I'm not interested in dredging it up now.

"I got it when I was thirteen during a football game." The scar is ugly, two inches in length with a knot in the middle and a thin red line that still runs the perimeter of it. For years, I waited in vain for the stripe to fade; now I welcome it, a reminder to never back down, to fight back, to never put myself in that kind of position again. The irony that a gunman had me cowering inside a windowless closet isn't lost on me.

"Want to tell me what happened?"

I shift in my seat to make room for hostility to join me on the sofa. "I already told you. A football game. In the middle of the third quarter." Yep, I hear it in my voice. Hostility and a fair amount of bitterness, but I don't give a damn. Who does he think he is, asking me these kinds of questions? I'm too old for this. The time for psycho-analysis came and went a long time ago.

"That doesn't look like any football injury I've seen before. You sure that's where it came from? You sure it wasn't a cut of some kind?" He looks down at his notebook, picks up his pen. I'm a statistic, and he knows it. And the scratch of a few words on paper is all it will take to make things official after all these years, unless you count my middle school counselor. Even she never came out and asked—just looked at me with pity and asked over and over and over if there was anything I needed to talk about.

I don't count her. Never have.

"Football game. Third-quarter." I recite the words on automatic, like the robot I've been trained to be for the last sixteen years. *Where'd you get that cut?* Football game. *Where'd you get that black eye?* Ran into a door. *Why's your hair wet?* Washed it. *In the bathroom?* Yep.

"Looks more like a knife blade caused it. Maybe a piece of glass." He's still looking at my arm. The guy won't let up, and I bristle. I made peace with my anger a long time ago, but he's intent on digging it up and I want no part of it. He tents his hands and looks up at me through hooded lashes, the ballpoint pen threaded between his fingers. "Or something else."

I rub the bump on my scar and look away, then curse myself for the tell. Eye contact is essential when trying to convince someone they're wrong, and I just failed the challenge. The worst part is, he guessed right. Bingo. Ding ding ding. Grab your door prize on the way out.

I remember the way my arm bled, the way Blake Jennings denied any wrongdoing. *"He tripped, Coach, like he always does. I didn't mean for it to happen."* I remember the laughs. The taunts from my teammates and the opposing team. I remember my coach's pat on the arm, his "there there, you can't help being small and uncoordinated" attitude as he pulled a handkerchief out of his pocket and wrapped it around my arm with a flippant "he lasted twenty seconds this time. Is that a record?" comment to the assistant coach as I walked away with the team manager and listened to both men laugh. I remember my mom's tears, my dad's outrage, my denial of the truth even as I stuffed it deep inside.

I remember the blood. So much blood. Blood on the grass, blood on my uniform. The cut required six stitches to close. My mother had a tough time removing the stain on my shirt.

I blink, all at once remembering where I am. My fists are clenched. Sweat dots my hairline. The counselor's gaze travels slowly between the two. He looks at me, one eyebrow raised, his mouth parted as if to question me further.

Screw his questions. I've sold out arenas and had four number one songs. I don't need to revisit a past that no longer matters. I came here to talk about the shooting and how to get back on stage. I did not come here to relive my awful childhood. If I'd wanted to see Dr. Phil, I would've reached out to Oprah.

I stand up with an, "I'm out," and walk out the door. I don't need therapy. I can deal with things on my own, the way I've always done. When you're a thirteen-year-old kid being pushed around by his classmates...being buried head-first inside a dirty, grimy toilet for ten, twenty, twenty-six God-awful seconds...you learn to deal. When your teammates—particularly one overgrown quarterback who picked on the small kids in order to feel big—trips you in the third quarter and uses his cleat to step on your arm and slide his foot two inches to the right...you learn to deal. When you're locked inside a locker-room closet after school and left there alone until a janitor finds you the next morning...you learn to deal. My parents called the cops on that one, but they couldn't find me. There were no cell phones to track when I was in seventh grade. I spent the night curled up next to a bag of soccer balls.

You don't go through that and come out of it unable to cope. I can cope. I've always coped. I'm a freaking entertainer, for heaven's sake. I've written hit songs on this topic and coped all the way to the bank.

My music saves people.

The fans tell me so.

Being locked inside a closet again nearly killed me in more ways than one.

If Jane hadn't been there, I wouldn't have made it out with my sanity intact.

With a jerk of the handle, I open the car door and climb inside. Two seconds later, my tires squeal out of the parking lot.

The last thing I see before pulling my Lexus onto the road is a vaguely familiar flash of long blonde hair from the sidewalk across the street. The sight jolts me for a moment, because for a second I think the person looks like...

My heart skids and bounces, but I'm too far away to get a good look.

I'm in Nashville, and she's in Seattle.

I keep driving.

CHAPTER FOURTEEN

Jane

Seattle comes by its reputation honestly. The city is known for its incessant love for rainy days and its uncanny ability to inflict depression on otherwise healthy people. And this week, both are working in tandem to spin their black magic on me.

It has rained for four days straight with no letup—not even the customary mid-afternoon reprieve to give people a chance to make a coffee run, haul their trash to the curb, go for a walk without having to come home wet. Coincidently, my tears have fallen for nearly as many days, save the workday lull when grown men are present. When other people are in the room, I somehow pull it together. When they walk out, the dam breaks loose, and I'm reapplying mascara on my lunch break.

That counselor. He couldn't have been more wrong if he had guessed I was a professional ballerina who also dabbles in woodworking, but that doesn't mean his words didn't affect me. That doesn't mean I haven't thought about them a hundred times since our last appointment.

I think you have some deep-seated issues to deal with.

I think most of them involve your baby.

I don't have baby issues.

"Jane, are you alright?"

Startled, I jump and drop the unopened Snickers bar I've just retrieved from my purse. Peyton, a petite curly-headed brunette who works loans and is my best work-friend, leans against the open breakroom door, sipping a can of Sprite through a straw.

"I'm fine." My voice cracks on the words, exposing the lie. As if the wetness on my cheeks wasn't enough of an indicator that I am, in fact, not fine. Five minutes until lunch break is over, and I haven't been able to keep my eyes dry long enough to fix myself. The last thing I want is to see the concerned face of yet another co-worker whose mind should be on business as usual—not on whether her best friend is on the verge of a mental breakdown.

She swallows. "You're not okay at all. Anything you want to talk about?"

I run two fingers under my eyes. "Not unless you have all day, and only if you promise not to charge me one-fifty an hour for your time." I sigh and turn toward the mirror hanging over the sink. It's worse than I thought. Even if I can get the black stuff off my skin, there's no hiding the redness unless I want to slip on a pair of sunglasses and look like a hungover sorority girl.

"You're going to counseling then. Thank goodness."

I shoot her a look. "He is a jerk, and I'm pretty sure he thinks I'm crazy. Nice to know you're happy about it."

"Oh, shut up." She rolls her eyes. "If I'd had a gun pointed at my head...if I were locked inside a closet...if I had seen the things you saw, I would be in counseling, too. As it stands, I sometimes go to help me kick my shoplifting habit."

I look at her, a big bite of chocolate in my mouth.

"I'm just trying to make you feel better," she says with a shrug.

I wad up the empty candy bar wrapper and reach for my water. "Try a little harder. What are you doing in here anyway? Don't you have money to hand out or something?"

"Not today. I was in the office photocopying papers, and they sent me down here to get you. There's someone here to see you."

I stop chewing and frown. Here? To see me? In the year since I started this job, no one has ever stopped by for a visit. I peer over at her. She's twirling a strand of curly hair around her index finger. Never a good sign.

"Who is it?" A ball of dread just pitched a tent inside my stomach.

"A man, but he didn't give a name. I think he might be a reporter."

"Oh, for heaven's sake. Because I don't return their calls, they decide to visit me at work?" I fling my trash into the bin and stomp toward the door, not stopping to analyze her concerned look on the way out. "That's harassment. Or invasion of privacy. Or something I haven't thought of yet."

I burst into the lobby, cringing a little when the door bounces against the glass wall. All eyes turn toward me, and then I scan the room.

I see a man I don't recognize standing near the back, holding a cell phone. He wears glasses and makes me think of Clark Kent; the look screams reporter. I make a determined path straight to him.

"Can I help you?" I say the words to be polite when in truth, I don't want to help him at all. I want him to leave. I want to leave. I want to go home and bury myself under my blankets and pretend the month of November never existed on the calendar.

"As a matter of fact, you can." He gives a single nod. I try not to notice then way every head in the office has turned our way. After the concert shooting, my co-workers watched the news. I think they all have a pretty good idea what he's doing here. "I'm Brian Daniel with the Seattle Times. I'm wondering if you have a comment about Teddy Hayes' recent meltdown on stage?" When I frown, he keeps going. "It's been all over the news. Is there any insight you might be able to give us on his state of mind? It seems like you probably know more than anyone what he's gone through, and—"

Meltdown?

"N...no." I stammer. "I don't have anything to say at all." I'm all at once confused and concerned, and both those emotions quickly morph into irritated and outraged. How dare he come all the way here to ask me something so personal. "Teddy is his own person, and I wouldn't presume to speak for him. If you want to know his state of mind, I suppose you should ask him. I'm afraid I can't help you."

"But if it's not too much trouble, could you—"

"Sorry, but it is too much trouble. I'm afraid you've wasted your time."

"Have you spoken with him since the incident? Would you mind if I—"

But I'm not listening. Right now, I'm not even interested in doing my job. No, I haven't spoken with him, and no, I haven't a clue about his state of mind. Unless it's anything like mine, in which case it's terrible. The only difference is, I can be a mess in private. No one needs to know.

I need a laptop and a quiet room.

I have no idea what that reporter is talking about, but I'm going to find out.

A few minutes later, I've read a dozen headlines and skimmed a handful of articles. Tiny cracks line the edges of my heart as it breaks just a little. One thin fissure manages to work its way straight through the middle, and the crying starts. It's amazing how many tears a person can shed for someone they barely know.

Oh, Teddy.

Teddy

You're such a loser.

Those four words have played through my mind all morning, words I've heard and fought against all my life, a monster on my tail just out of reach. The faster I go, the better the chance I have to outrun them forever. Last night the monster caught me. He still has me in his grip.

I lost.

Last night, in front of eighteen thousand people, and God knows how many others who've watched it online, I lost. The internet doesn't need ticket sales or viewership numbers to up the Neilsen ratings. I'm the number one trending topic on Twitter; there's a YouTube video out there that's been viewed over three million times, and it's only been twelve hours.

Twelve hours since I froze. Twelve hours since I sang the last line of our opening song and began the second. I knew I was done for the second I climbed inside that crane and began the ascent; an ascent I've practiced more than a hundred times without a single hitch.

But the moment it began to rise upward with me inside, I scanned the crowd. Any glint of silver made me flinch. Someone took a photo with a flash, and I ducked. The song lyrics I've known for more than a year completely disappeared, like steam rising over boiling water. There one second, gone the next. In the video, you can hear me saying, "Get me down!" over and over. At first, it's only a panicked whisper. Within seconds, it morphs into a loud tantrum, like I didn't care who heard it. The crane was lowered and I climbed out, then spent the next thirty seconds trying to catch my breath, slow my erratic heartbeat; attempting to squeak out the next words and finally walking off the stage.

I remember glancing at my arm, fully expecting to see a gash from a football cleat. My past fear and my current fear had slammed headlong in a battle for dominance. Neither won. I definitely lost.

The audience—to their credit—went silent. Ten, maybe twenty people began to boo, but they were quickly chastised and stopped. Eighteen thousand people waited around a good half hour, but I couldn't bring myself to return. It was like the fans felt my fear and accepted it. Understood it, even. They never once made demands on my time. That part, at least, means a lot.

That touching show of support won't last forever. A few days at most. Not enough time for an already scheduled tour with eleven remaining cities that soon extends to five countries in Europe and a special Christmas performance in Nashville. I'm not sure I'll manage to show up for any of them.

People get shot when they come to see me, and I can't be responsible for compromising the safety of so many. I won't be.

Not to mention that every time I close my eyes, a man I can't see points a gun to my head. I wake up before he pulls the trigger. The vision is so real, that on the nights I'm lucky enough to fall asleep at all, I jolt awake sweating profusely and fighting with the sheets. The lack of rest leaves me exhausted. The paranoia makes me certain I'm going crazy. If I haven't lost my mind yet, I'm well on my way.

How am I supposed to get on stage again when just thinking about it makes my heart race and my limbs shake? My nails are bitten off, and my resting heart rate can't be healthy. Tomorrow night I'm supposed to be in Flagstaff. The odds of me actually showing up aren't looking good, not if last night is any indication.

I'm afraid to perform.

It's the most hopeless I've felt in my life, worse even than the way it felt when an entire football team and two coaches laughed at me in front of a stadium filled with hometown spectators. And that's saying a lot.

Liam isn't home, so I grab my keys and go for a run.

The weather is chilly. My breath escapes in front of me in tiny cloudbursts that spread across my forehead as I move through them, but I keep going. My neighborhood is a series of curves and inclines that make even a car shudder and jerk in the effort to navigate around them. My gray Lexus seems relieved every night when I finally pull into a parking space and shut it off for the evening.

I'm shivering before I make it down the street. I pull the hood over my head and yank my jacket's zipper all the way up, then turn right and head uphill. Normally I head left, out to the main road, but it feels good to push myself. This is how I deal with frustration, and lately it's been served up with abundance.

I want to see Jane. When I'm not thinking about getting shot, I'm thinking about her. There was something calming about her that I've never known before or since. I can't shake the feeling that if I could see her, things might get better. There's only one problem.

She has a boyfriend.

Which means things will continue to stay worse.

———

Jane

"That guy is messed up."

I startle, surprised to hear Ben behind me when I didn't

notice he'd come into the bedroom. I steal a glance at the clock: 8:00 pm. I haven't eaten dinner. Instead, I've been on my bed, hunched over my computer for nearly two hours, watching YouTube clips and reading article after article detailing Teddy's meltdown. He seemed fairly composed until the part where he barked the words, "Get me down." Where most of the audience stared in shock, I imagined what it felt like to haul him over the side and began to cry. I'm surprised he climbed into the lift in the first place. An overwhelming desire to rescue him again comes at me in a rush.

I quickly swipe at my eyes before turning to look at Ben.

"It was a pretty harrowing experience. It would mess anyone up."

Ben half-laughs over my shoulder before sitting on the edge of my bed. "Yeah, but he's a guy. You gotta toughen up and get over it eventually."

"Says the guy who's never been held at gunpoint," I say, not even bothering to keep the sarcasm out of my tone. "It's been a week."

"It's not like he was shot, Jane. That..." he twirls a finger toward my computer screen, "is a little much, don't you think? Everyone was talking about it at work. All I know is, if I made a million dollars a night, I'd get over it pretty quick."

"He's not making a million dollars a night," I snap, feeling defensive for no good reason. "What were they saying?" I want to know, but I don't. I like the guys we work with, and I'd rather things stay that way.

"Just that he looked weak. Maybe faking it a little. You know what they say. When you're a celebrity, all publicity is good publicity. They've probably figured out a way to keep this going for a while so he can stay in the news."

I take it back; I now hate everyone we work with except for Andy. At the moment, even Ben is included in that mix. We've been dating for nearly a year, my longest relationship to date. I once had a reputation as a serial dater, something my friends and I used to laugh about, make wagers on, even. I was the only one whose laughter was part of the act. Commitment doesn't come easily for me, not after the baby. Once you're labeled a whore and subsequently get your heart broken—I suppose one loss wasn't enough for my sixteen-year-old self—it's hard to trust anyone. What if you open up and get destroyed for it? Self-vulnerability can be another person's weapon to use against you.

Before Ben, my dating record was eighteen days, which makes Ben and I practically engaged at this point. But this is the first time I've seen his jealous side, unless you count the time his best friend bought a scratch-off lottery ticket right after him at a convenience store in Lynwood. Ben won five dollars. He was excited until Ricky won a thousand. All I heard for a solid month was how Ben was behind him in line, but Ricky let him go first, as though the whole thing was a giant set-up to make him lose.

This feels similar, except how can he possibly be jealous of a man whose arena was shot up, resulting in the death of five people?

"He's not faking it. Tell the guys to lay off."

Ben makes an affronted noise. "Whose side are you on?"

I open a new website without looking up. "I wasn't aware there were sides."

"I'm just saying. Theoretically—if there were sides—whose side would you be on?"

I shut my computer and look Ben in the eye. There's no way I can talk about this without getting into another discussion I don't want to have. "I'm on the side of whoever was trapped in that arena, scared to death they might get shot. That includes Teddy, me, Andy, and fifteen thousand other people whose names I don't even know. If that means I'm not on your side, then so be it. But frankly, it bothers me that you're even talking about sides when you weren't there. There are no sides, Ben. So stop trying to pit me against you. And please stop making fun of Teddy. He's a guy who's rattled, that's it. He shouldn't be the butt of anyone's joke, not right now."

Ben blinks, his mouth going slack before it slowly hardens. I'm looking at the jealous face again, and I don't know why.

"Wow, someone's very defensive of a guy she claims not to know much."

"I'm not defensive, I just—"

"I think we need to take a little break in conversation here." He stands up, rubs his hands together, then flexes his fingers a couple times. "I'm going to head home and watch the game. I might be back later, or maybe I'll wait until tomorrow. I just need some time..."

"What's this about?" I say, not ready to cower from his overt passive aggression. "Is it that hard to understand why I might have a problem with you poking fun at someone who had a public panic attack on stage, Ben? I feel bad for him. This whole thing hasn't been easy."

He holds up his hands in mock surrender. "I don't feel bad for him. Teddy Hayes is a grown man with a job to do, and he's failing at it. He needs to grow up and get over himself."

You're jealous. I think the words, but I don't say them out loud.

"So out of curiosity, what you're saying is, if I have a meltdown at any time in the future, I would also need to 'get over myself?'"

"Now you're making this about you," he mutters, rolling his eyes.

"It is about me." I look up at him, wishing that for once in my life someone would allow me to be human. To mess up. To cry and grieve and be afraid and feel the weight of loss and still be welcomed anyway. Then again, maybe my words are more accurate than I thought. Maybe this is about me. Maybe I keep choosing people who judge harshly because I've never stopped judging myself. "But you're right. You should probably go."

And that's what Ben does, making sure to slam the door so I hear it loud and clear.

I lie back on the bed, wondering why I've done this for so long. It feels a little bit like wasting my life, though I can't pinpoint anything that actually helps me draw that conclusion. I love Ben, I think. But if I'm being honest...we're competitive. I keep him at arm's length, and he knocks me down with digs and backhanded compliments. He likes affection, but I don't. He's passive-aggressive and I'm just passive, if passive means slightly self-loathing and too numb to care about much, including myself. The only thing we have in common is our job. I'm not sure that's enough to hold together a relationship.

Funny that I never once shied away from Teddy's closeness.

But the issue here isn't Teddy. It's Ben and me together.

Specifically, me being in the spotlight. I like fading into the background while Ben likes being the star of the show. And now I've brushed shoulders with the famous Teddy Hayes, and have been in the news all week for my specific brand of 'heroics.' Reporters used that word, not me. I kept him alive. I kept him company. I kept him hidden and out of harm's way. For that, I'm called a hero and the media hasn't let up. Every time another news story shows up online or on television, Ben bristles.

And that, friends, is the wrap-up of our current relationship status.

I stare toward the door, wondering if he'll walk back through while simultaneously hoping he doesn't. How many years of my life have I spent thinking this same thought about every man I've dated? Worse, how many more years will I spend in the future? I haven't let anyone in since my high school boyfriend, and that ended horribly. We've only had one conversation about marriage. A conversation that wasn't serious and concluded with no impending wedding date. The worst thing is, I'm okay with it. Something tells me healthy women in loving relationships wouldn't be.

You know that saying about how you should live your life and not let it live you? Lately, I've wondered if I'm doing the opposite. Shame buries a person deep when it has had ten years to pile on.

I blink and come out of my trance-like state. The door hasn't opened, and sitting here wondering if it will isn't going to solve my problems. My private life is a tangled mess of grief, comfortability, routine, and a few uncertain feelings that should undoubtedly be very certain by now. But dwelling on my life won't fix it right now. There's only one thing I can fix, or at least try to.

Scooting back on the bed, I open my laptop and reach for my phone.

———

Teddy

What happened? The text simply says, as though it doesn't shock the hell out of me and send my heart into my throat at the same time. She sent me a message. I didn't think she would. Ignoring the way my will to live just quadrupled times a hundred, I text back.

I choked in front of everyone. Sweet, simple, casual, the truth.

I saw that, she replies, effectively draining away whatever was left of my ego. I was kinda hoping she hadn't.

You and the rest of Twitter, YouTube, and the 5 o'clock news. It should be in People Magazine *tomorrow if you want to grab a copy.*

I don't, but thanks. Where are you now? She texts back.

Flagstaff. I have a concert tomorrow. I doubt I'll be able to perform, but I leave that part out.

Think you'll be able to perform? So much for leaving things out. It's been a long time since a stranger could see right through me. But that's just it, isn't it? Jane isn't a stranger. In the oddest way, it feels like she knows me better than anyone. When someone sees you at your worst, it's when you learn the most. Women—and some men—like the idea of me and nothing else. Any preconceived notions Jane had about me were smashed on literal impact. The moment she pulled me into that closet, all pretense was stripped away in the fight to stay alive. The number of times I gripped her hand was the best indication. You can't grip someone's hand through trauma without imprinting at least a part of yourself on them. I held her so much that I imprinted nearly everything I had, the good and the bad. Most people only see the false good. Jane saw the real terrible. I didn't even bother to hide it, so why start now?

Honestly, no. Again, why bother?

That's unfortunate. Mind if we keep talking for a while? Maybe it will help. I don't ask if she means for her or me. It won't help me, but I don't say that. I want to keep texting her. In this singular case, lying seems to be a necessary evil. A questionable means to the very best end.

Maybe it will. It doesn't, but we keep texting for nearly two hours.

Like I said, the very best end.

CHAPTER FIFTEEN

Jane

I have barely stepped inside my apartment when I hear it: a muffled ping coming from the inside of my bag. And it's not the first one or the second or even the third. When it comes to texting, Teddy is persistent, something I wasn't aware of when we were locked up. I would find his behavior a bit annoying if it didn't feel so sweet. A man hasn't cared this much about me in years. That thought pokes me in the conscience.

Ben cares, even if he hasn't spoken to me in two days. Right?

Shouldn't I be sure?

I press the questions down with a fist, deciding it isn't fair to have them at all when Ben isn't here to defend them. I push the front door closed with my hip, toss my purse on the tiny kitchen table, and kick off my shoes. Even low-top Converse can hurt after a while. I think there's a blister forming on my heel and possibly another on my right toe.

I limp a little on my way into the kitchen, then retrieve a water bottle from the refrigerator and unscrew the top, recalling the way my heart nearly leaped out of my chest when I witnessed Teddy's public meltdown. I've watched the video at least twenty times now. In jeans and a black sweater, he looked so much like the man I dragged into the closet, the GQ guy who turned out to be both friendly and fearsome, especially at the beginning.

Feeling a sudden wave of sadness at the memories, I hobble into the bedroom and remove my earrings and bracelet, tossing them onto my dresser, then snatch the phone out of my bag and fall onto my bed. My mother used to scold me for this. *Never lunge for a bed. You'll break the rails in the attempt to break your fall.* Those words never made sense to me, not then and not now. Whether or not anything breaks, it still leaves me lying prone in exhaustion at the end of the day, which is really all that matters.

I flip onto my back and read Teddy's three—no, four texts. Trying hard to ignore the way my heart suddenly picks up speed, I begin to type.

Yes, I had a good day today and no, there's no chance of me sleeping. I hardly do anymore. What's on your mind?

That first part was a white lie, but white also stands for purity. It's how I justify it. My day involved escorting some glitzy YouTube star to a fashion event in the city and listening to various make-up tutorials all afternoon. Did you know highlighters can really help your cheeks pop and give you a glow that lasts well into the evening? Well, so will sweat and wearing a bullet-proof vest all day while listening to YouTubers talk fashion.

My little white lie seems appropriate, considering the circumstances.

I stare at my phone, waiting for the three little dots of approval to appear that indicate he's working on a response. Nothing. I continue to stare, certain they'll appear any second. One, four, fifteen, sixty seconds go by. Nothing. The man can send text after text, but he can't respond to the one single one I've sent him? I lay there, increasingly frustrated and angry and hurt—all those emotions lobbed at me one after another until I'm juggling them with shaky hands and dropping them all over the place. Eventually, they shatter, and all I wind up feeling is depressed and inadequate. When do you finally and fully move past the mistakes of childhood and the mark they make?

Five minutes. It's been five minutes.

Ten years. It's been ten years.

I'm done.

Standing with a huff and trying not to cry—irrational, I know—I yank my shirt over my head and toss it on the floor, then head for the shower. This day has been crap, my hair smells like fifteen different types of perfume, my feet hurt, and I'm filled with a sudden need to rinse the residue away right along with the memories.

The water is running at the perfect close-to-boiling temperature when I hear it. A ping. Followed by another. Standing there half-naked and shivering, I debate climbing in and ignoring him altogether. But of course, the part of me that misses him despite the awful circumstances surrounding the way we met...the part of me that needs desperately to connect with someone—with Teddy, because who am I kidding? He's the only one I want to talk to—that part shuts off the shower and heads for my bed. The sound of gurgling water sliding down a partially clogged drain follows me as I snatch up the comforter, wrap it around my shoulders, and bury myself underneath it.

I read Teddy's newest text and smile.

And then I respond.

———

Teddy

I toss my phone onto the pillow next to me and stare at the ceiling. It's two a.m., and we've been texting since midnight. It's been ten minutes since I sent my last text to Jane and she still hasn't answered me. Something tells me she fell asleep despite her claim that she wouldn't. I know I'm selfish for wanting her to stay awake, but nighttime is the worst. I've never been afraid of the dark in my life, but I am now, struggling with monsters in the closet for the first time in my life. It's pathetic, but here we are.

Still, my last text was an important one, and I'd hoped to get a reaction. I was hoping she shared my struggle. Not knowing will keep me awake all night.

I push back my white down comforter and sit up, stretching my arms over my head. Bare-chested and cold, I make my way into the kitchen to grab a beer. Not the best thing to drink in the middle of the night, but the odds of sleeping were shot to hell the moment my agent called and told me fans were beginning to place bets on whether I'll show tomorrow night. I'm jittery and anxious because I can almost guarantee I won't. What if my career is finished? What if I can't ever get onstage again?

I pop the tab on the can and lean against the sink, looking around at the spacious apartment.

I don't rent; I own the place outright. All the stainless appliances and granite countertops and slate floors belong to me. In a couple years, thanks to a few extra payments on my part, and a little help from the guys, it will be one-hundred percent official. Not that I care all that much. I bought the place two years ago because my agent said I needed a safer place to live. I agreed to it without second-guessing him, though I can't pretend my ego wasn't involved in the sale. It was with a fair amount of pride and self-congratulation that I signed on the dotted line—a ten-year mortgage that I'm paying off much earlier, a payment more than triple in size from my last apartment, for more space than a bachelor needs all to himself.

It isn't exactly that I regret buying the apartment now. It's just that I know what happens to a person after the newness wears off. Instead of the high hopes you placed in your decision, you're left with a fresh kind of emptiness, one that isn't assuaged by shiny newness and fancy decorations.

In all the time I've lived here, I've never seen that six-burner stove used once. I believe in take-out, and the guys don't know how to work it. We tried to figure it out early on, but all we got was clicking noises and the faint scent of gas, so we shut it off quickly. Who owns so many nice things they never even touch?

Suddenly feeling despondent, I toss the half-empty beer can into the trash and make my way to the window. The view is unparalleled, stars for miles and lights of the city twinkling below me like a year-round holiday. It's Christmas at its best. A Norman Rockwell painting designed just for me. Yet it's doing nothing to improve my mood. Why hasn't Jane texted back? Why does it matter so much?

I try to work up some enthusiasm for the view because it is beautiful. It isn't common to everyone, and I'm lucky. Blessed, even. Proud winner of the apartment lottery jackpot and I need to be more grateful. I'm right on the verge of convincing myself I really do love this place when my phone chimes from the other room.

To heck with the view. I smile to myself at the idea of finally hearing from her and pick up the phone.

Sometimes I wish I could go back, just for a minute. That's a weird thing to admit, but it wasn't all bad.

I stare at her words, relating to them and memorizing them. She would go back, same as me. It's weird and it isn't, and no one else in the world would understand that strange, messed-up catch-twenty-two but her. I make myself respond, even though I know it might open a door I won't ever be able to close completely.

So would I. For a minute. Maybe a few more. I don't regret everything.

The phone sits like fire in my hands. Feelings burn when they first come out, even if they come out as a tiny spark. I'm talking about the kiss, and we both know it. Sure I kissed her, but that action could always be blamed on last-minute desperation. The words I just typed expose way more than the kiss ever did; more than it seems on paper. Thoughts. Fears. Feelings. A whole bunch of tangled emotions, I can't even begin to unwind. Jane might not recognize them for what they are. But I know she will.

My gut churns when she doesn't respond right away. What is she thinking? Is she mad? Should I have kept everything to myself? I'm contemplating a nice enough way to backtrack when another chime finally comes through.

I have nightmares. So many of them. It's the reason I hate to sleep.

I stare at the message for a long time, trying to gauge her meaning. But then I know...she's giving me an out. It's one I don't want to take, but I appreciate the effort. Still, time might not be a bad thing. I once read that if you go too fast, you break things. I don't want to break this, even if it never goes beyond simple friendship. I roll with the new direction she's veered and type back.

What do you dream about? She immediately begins typing, though the message must be a long one.

The shoes lying around the arena. The kid in the closet with us. The gun. "Say It." That stupid game keeps rolling through my mind. I have so many better questions I could have asked if I'd thought about them at the time.

Despite the serious subject, that makes me smile.

You can always ask now.

Okay, I will. Do you...like to go camping?

I laugh and type a response. ***That's the better question you would have asked me? Not what I expected. But yes, I like to go camping.***

It's an important question, and I needed to know the answer.

Why? Do you love camping or something?

No, I hate it. I'd have to sleep on the ground and use the bathroom in a bucket or something. I'll camp at a Ramada Inn, thank you very much.

Ramada Inn? That's her idea of a nice hotel? I smile at her simplicity, even while considering the over-the-top opulence of my own apartment.

Then I guess I'll never ask you to go camping with me. You'd turn me down flat based on the bathroom facilities alone.

I wait, the phone resting in my palm like a lottery ticket one scratch away from winning. Once again, she's gone silent. Once again, I'm holding my breath. And once again, I'm second-guessing the wisdom of my words. Maybe my innuendo is too much all at once. Maybe I should back off, leave her alone, give it my best shot at drifting back to the normal I knew before I met Jane.

But then a text comes through.

I might consider it. I would just need some time to think.

I blink at her response, unable to think past her implication. I don't answer her. I have no idea what to say, because I don't think we're talking about camping any longer. Jane has a lot to think about, things I don't even have to consider. I need to remember that right now, we're just friends. Friends who've gone through a particularly crippling circumstance together, yes. But still friends.

I sit at the edge of my bed for the next two hours, analyzing that friendship while trying not to think of the monsters still in the closet...ready and waiting to pounce.

CHAPTER SIXTEEN

Jane

I might consider it.

I barely slept last night. What was I thinking? I practically threw myself at the guy over text, though he was too decent to point it out. Unlike me, who isn't decent at all. I have a boyfriend, one I'm currently waiting for at a coffee shop across from Pike's Market downtown. It's nearly noon, and I've been here twenty minutes already. He's a little late, but I was a little early, so I suppose the two even out somehow. I sip my pumpkin latte and stare out the window, watching for him, and working to up my holiday mood. The day is unseasonably warm, and by warm, I mean the sun is making a rare appearance and temperatures are hovering in the high fifties.

People are milling everywhere, carrying bouquets of flowers from the fish market in one hand, and paper Starbucks cups from the original store just down the street in the other . Tourists don't know about this place, thank God. I mean, I frequent Starbucks like every other patriotic American, but you'll never catch me standing in that particular line.

I sigh, depressed by the flowers and the coffee...depressed by life in general, actually. Loss and near-death experiences cause you to reevaluate your life, but rather than accentuating everything that makes you thankful, it highlights everything wrong. I've lived inside a decade of wrong, but I'm just now starting to face it. Instead of feeling enlightened, I'm sad. Becoming aware of your own character flaws isn't always as empowering as you think, at least not at first. I roll my cup between both palms and take another sip.

There's still no sign of Ben; he's now twenty minutes late.

Thanksgiving is next week, and I feel about as thankful as one might feel after stepping in chewed gum or dog poo. Why do bad things happen to good people? A cliché for sure, but it turns out it's oddly appropriate.

I catch a flash of red, recognizing Ben's jacket before I see his face. He pushes through the front door and meets my carefully controlled gaze. I'm annoyed and working hard not to show it. A small smile helps, I think, though it feels a little too forced. I stand and kiss him on the cheek and am greeted with a rigid jaw I choose to ignore.

"What took you so long?" I ask, inserting a lightness into my tone that I don't feel.

"I've been thinking. Walking around the block, making sure what I wanted to say before I walked in," he says, sitting across from me without smiling. I see the hurt in his eyes and the resignation. Emotion makes it hard for me to respond because I know what's coming. It's the way every relationship ends with me. I'm emotionally unavailable, physically detached, incapable of letting anyone in. It's all true, but I wish it weren't. My baggage has taken a seat between us and will not leave quietly. I know this from experience.

As for Ben, he's never wanted to acknowledge the baggage or carry any of it for me. Maybe if the bags weren't so heavy, our relationship wouldn't strain from all the effort.

"Okay." I shrug and reach for my latte to have something to do. "I thought maybe you got held up by something."

Ben glances out the window. "I ran into a buddy of mine from college in front of the market. He wanted to hear all about the shooting and how you're doing. He was impressed with how you handled things." There's no inflection in his words.

"What did you say?"

"I said you were fine, but I'm not sure that's true." He rubs his hands together and stands up. "Still, I can't wait for the day when people aren't constantly asking me about it. Doesn't look like it will happen anytime soon." He walks to the counter to order a drink, and I watch. I take in his mannerisms, his smile, his lean in her direction, and then his head shake, his hands that flail when she says something he doesn't like. I look away, uncomfortable with the judgment I'm sending. They say not to let outsiders into your relation-ship, and maybe that's what I'm doing, comparing him unfairly to someone else. I pull out my phone and consider deleting my texts with Teddy, innocent enough as they are. Possibly deleting his number altogether. I hold it in my palm and weigh the pros and cons, fully aware of the heaviness that settles around me when I make the decision to delete.

"You're never gonna believe what she wanted to know." Ben falls into the chair across from me. It scrapes against the tile floor with a loud screech.

"What?" I ask cautiously, setting my phone down. I'll delete the messages later.

"If you were the girl from the news. And if you could introduce her to Teddy Hayes, as though you're best friends with him now or something."

I glance at the barista, who excitedly waves at me. "The answer to that question is no," I say, my eyes once again on Ben.

He just stares at me. "That's what I told her, but she barely listened." Instead, he mimics her. "'Is she the girl from the news? Does she know Teddy Hayes? Did you know your girlfriend is a hero?'"

That last one bothers me. I take a breath, then another, thinking. Thinking.

"You're really annoyed by all this, aren't you? You know I was just doing my job, right? That I would do it again if I had to?"

"That's what I'm afraid of," he mutters.

"Meaning? You want me to quit?"

He picks up his mug and blows across the top of the foam. "I didn't say quit. Just...stop taking so many high-profile jobs."

I look at him. "That's the only high-profile job I've ever gotten."

He takes a sip and swallows loudly. "Yet it sure worked out for you, didn't it?"

That's it. My blood is boiling hotter than my latte. "Actually, it worked out pretty poorly from my perspective. I can't sleep, can't even close my eyes without imagining a gun pointed at me. I can't shower without jumping out every time I hear a noise. I'm afraid to walk alone at night, not the most convenient thing for a security guard. There's a list. Want to hear more?"

Ben sighs. "Look, I'm not saying I don't want you to work. I'm just saying—"

"That the high-profile cases should only belong to you?"

He doesn't say anything, and I know that's exactly what he's thinking. Everything in me stills, and I stare. It's a rough transition, the moment you see your past life intersect with your future life at a place where they can no longer coexist, especially when so much of that past life is tied to a person. My life has been tied to Ben for nearly a year. It's been good...

but not good enough, because good enough is what I've told myself to settle for. Good enough for the girl who got pregnant. Good enough for the girl who ruined the pastor's kid. Good enough for the girl who couldn't save her baby. Good enough for the girl who got kicked out of church. Good enough for the girl buried in shame she thought she deserved. But this is the moment.

This is the moment.

And it has absolutely nothing to do with Teddy Hayes. Whether I see that man or any other man ever again, my life is here, and this is what I need to do. I deserve more than my own beat-downs. I was brave last week, and it's time to start being brave now. So before I lose the nerve, I open my mouth and say it.

"Ben, it's time for us to break up."

A tiny part of my heart dies at the surprised look on his face.

But not nearly as much as it should.

———

Teddy

One of my very first concerts was held at the Pepsi Amphitheater in Flagstaff, and my memories of it are nearly incomparable. It was the first show I opened for a major act —Kenny Chesney, to be exact. I was as green as the grass on the sprawling lawn and scared out of my mind. I've dealt with stage-fright at every point in my career, but it reached the stuck-in-a-locker-room-closet level that night. Still, that show was a turning point, the first time I felt that nod in my subconscious that I was going to make it and make it big. For this tour, I wanted to come back to this venue out of a mix of nostalgia and respect. It's a smaller venue than the rest, but I owed these people nearly everything, and I wanted to pay them back.

Now they're screaming my name, and I'm paralyzed in place.

I can't go out there.

The fright I felt that night all those years ago was nothing compared to now, because now it's a fear for my life. Even more, a fear for everyone's life in the stands, knowing I'm responsible for anything that might go wrong. The thought of getting on that stage...of anyone being harmed...I can't do it. *Here I go again* is one of the worst feelings in the world when you're powerless to stop it.

"You ready?" Jack says, popping his head in my dressing room. He looks at me sitting barefoot in front of the dressing room table, still in sweatpants and a t-shirt, and cautiously steps inside. He closes the door behind him. "What's going on, bud?"

I scrub both hands through my hair and lock them behind my head, then look up at him.

"I can't." Two simple words that affect everyone around me. I'm thirteen years old and the Teddy Hayes from last week all rolled into one. It's the worst part of headline entertaining that no one tells you about; the livelihood of dozens of people rests on your shoulders whether you're prepared to handle it or not. A sick day for me means a smaller paycheck for everyone else. But I'm not sick, I'm petrified. The weight of ten-thousand people sits on both of my shoulders, and I can't shake it off. I couldn't shake it off even if Taylor Swift screamed the words in my face. My memories won't let me. I've been bargaining with them all afternoon.

Jack lowers himself to the floor with a long, labored sigh. We don't speak because there isn't much to say. Eventually, he comes up with something. Jack isn't one for silence.

"I get it, Teddy. I was there that night too, remember? But

you've got to go up there and perform. A couple nights were fine; everyone understood. I'm not sure they will again."

"I don't need them to understand." I take a deep breath. "I'm not sure I'll be able to perform again. If that's the case, it won't matter what they think."

Jack laughs, but there's no humor behind it. "You'll perform again, sooner than you think. Just come out here with me, and we'll rip off the bandage together."

I want to, I really do. I'm fully aware that not going makes me weak and cowardly, but that's like telling a depressed person to snap out of it because of everything they should be thankful for. Thanks for that, got it. But it doesn't help at all. I know I'm weak and cowardly; I was told that every day from fourth to twelfth grade. The difference between then and now is, now I'm okay with it if it means everyone stays alive.

Five people dead. It's the headline that follows my name every time anyone talks about me.

"Musician Teddy Hayes, the country singer whose concert was sold out last week when five people were killed..."

Five people.

Including two children.

Including one person still on life support. Most likely, they'll bring the total to seven.

Not an easy thing to have on your resume. I certainly never asked for it and never will again.

"Go on out, and I'll be there in a few," I say to Jack.

He pats me on the leg in an *I knew you could do it* gesture, and stands up. I watch him go. When he closes the door, I reach for my wallet and phone and shove both into my pocket. I saw the Exit door across the hall from my dressing room. As soon as Jack's footsteps fade, I sneak out of the room and into the night air. All around me, music blares, and fans shout my name in a pounding chant.

Teddy.

Teddy.

Teddy.

The sound reminds me of gunshots. *Boom boom. Boom boom. Boom boom.*

They think he was targeting Teddy himself...

Cowardly or not, that won't happen again on my watch.

I jog down the street and round a corner, then call for an Uber. It arrives three minutes later, and we pull away from the venue. When the driver asks where we're going, I just tell him to drive.

He stays on the clock three hours before heading back to the hotel. I have no idea where we went; I spent most of the drive with my eyes closed, trying to settle my heart rate and my over-active imagination. I pay him in cash and walk up to my room.

If anyone knows I'm here, they never say anything about it. Then again, I fly home before the sun comes up and don't give them the chance.

———

Jane

I've cried for twenty-four straight hours, except for the five hours I managed to sleep. But even then, I dreamed I was crying. In it, I lost a friend's baby while shopping in Target, even though the only friend I have with kids is a mom to a seven-year-old boy. Hardly a baby. It was a stupid dream.

My waking hours have been stupid, as well. I've second-guessed myself every minute of them. *I shouldn't have broken up with Ben. I should have broken up with Ben a long time ago. The days after trauma are not the days to make life-altering decisions. But if not then, when is the right time?* If life does indeed flash before your eyes, are you not supposed to change the things you see

as wrong when you're given a second chance? I haven't
allowed myself a real second chance in a decade, instead
choosing punishment, routine, and a near-emotionless exis-
tence. This time my life flashed and I reacted. Foolish or not,
the decision was made. I mostly don't regret it.

Until all the in-between moments when I do.

Until my mind inadvertently slides to Teddy Hayes. One
thing I do know—besides knowing the break up was the right
thing to do—is that relationships built from trauma never
make it. I'm attracted to Teddy because we survived a crisis
and nothing more. Our friendship is shallow at best, even if it
feels real. The mind is a master of trickery; it uses the heart
to get its point across, like the manipulator it is.

Teddy Hayes is not the reason I broke up with Ben, even
if the memory of him has grown a bit.

I vow not to think of him anymore and reach for my
phone to call Andy. I'm supposed to work security tonight at
the Crocodile, but I'm not feeling well. A broken heart probably isn't the right ailment to claim, so I go with headache
and beg tonight off. It works. With a night to myself, I pull
up the number for Kin Dee and order delivery. Thai noodles
with chicken will be here in an hour, which leaves me a
decent amount of time to take a bath and search for something to watch on Netflix. I reach for my phone again—why
are phones equal parts blessing and curse?—to search for a
show when I accidentally click on Twitter and see the
headline.

Teddy Hayes A No-Show Again. And under the headline?
*Fans Beginning to Worry About His Mental Health in the Wake of
Recent Shooting.*

My chest caves in on itself as I read, both sick and sad for
him and the backlash he's sure to face this time. The article is
written from an angle that's surprisingly compassionate and
concerned, and includes interviews with a handful of

survivors, all of whom express the same fears and insecurities as Teddy. Afraid to be in public, afraid of loud noises, afraid of getting shot. The article in and of itself is fair. Most of the comments underneath the link are not.

I paid good money to see this loser, and I want a refund.

Get over yourself, dude.

Celebrities think the world revolves around them.

As far as I'm concerned, Teddy Hayes is officially canceled.

I haven't heard from Teddy in two days, but I quickly pull up his number. I hesitate a second, weighing the pros and cons of texting him at all, considering my newfound vow not to think of him anymore. What did that last, maybe three seconds? With an eye roll that defies any Ben ever threw my way, I begin typing a message. I try to tell myself I'm simply a concerned friend, but my pounding heart isn't having any of that nonsense right now.

You okay?

The thing I hate about texting is that it only takes ten seconds or so to pass before you start feeling paranoid. *Am I annoying? Does he want me to leave him alone? Am I nothing more than an overbearing, slightly psychotic fan? Oh my gosh, he hates me. Why couldn't I leave well enough alone?*

At thirty seconds, I'm second-guessing every life decision I've ever made and considering blocking his number just to avoid embarrassment. But then at forty, the blessed three dots appear. I wish we could all go back to talking. At least then, you didn't project your own insecurities onto other people just because they needed a moment to think.

No. I'm a failure at my job. If I even have a job anymore.

My heart squeezes at the uncertainty in his words.

You'll have a job after this. You just need to get back on stage.

This time his text is immediate.

That's the problem. I can't.

I chew a fingernail. He's in worse shape than I thought, and I knew it was bad. Of course, it's bad; the entire situation was awful. But now I'm more concerned. Giving up on an entire career is crazy, which makes me wonder at his mental state. I've been suffering, some days worse than others, but I haven't considered quitting my job. It makes me think Teddy honestly blames himself.

I blink at a sofa cushion.

That's it, Teddy blames himself. And not in an offhanded, "I feel bad" way. But in a way that shoulders the blame for the lives of five people being snuffed out in an instant. I haven't thought about quitting my job because I haven't—not for one second—felt as though I could have stopped it. But Teddy... he's analyzing and guilt-tripping himself into a downward spiral of false responsibility. Guilt is a burden we aren't meant to bear, yet Teddy is wrapped in it like a second skin he can't shed.

I sit with my phone, unable to think of a way to respond. Years ago, I watched an old movie, I didn't like, but still remember all these years later. In it, a psychologist takes on a phobia-ridden male client who takes co-dependent neediness to a new level—following the doctor on vacations, to family dinners, calling him at inappropriate times; literally, everywhere the doctor goes, the patient shows up. Nowadays, people would get arrested for this sort of stalker behavior, but back then, people quickly took to the neurotic patient... everyone except the doctor.

He wanted his life back.

He wanted to be left alone.

He wanted crazy Bob to get the heck away from him.

So he introduced the concept of baby steps. Baby steps toward separating himself from the doctor's family. Baby steps toward living his own life. Baby steps toward moving beyond fear of leaving the house. In the doctor's professional opinion, baby steps were the key to everything.

Teddy isn't neurotic and hardly has a fear of living, but he clearly has a fear of something.

Baby steps.

Maybe a few steps up and back are what he needs to be able to fully move forward.

Maybe it's a ridiculous idea, but it's the only one I've got.

You're not quitting your job. A bold demand to make to someone I just met, but I'm serious. He's not.

I'm not, huh? Well, it's going to be hard to perform when I can't get on stage.

I read the message, then read it again, aware that he's serious. Then again, so am I.

Where are you?

I'm home. I have the next few days off the tour, though it might as well be four years at this point.

I sigh, hating the dejected tone I hear in his words. I pull down Teddy's text thread and open the dial screen. The first thing I do is call my boss and ask for a few days off.

Then I call a work friend and ask for a favor. Two actually.

And then I buy a plane ticket.

The next time Teddy Hayes has a meltdown, he'll have to do it in front of me.

———

Teddy

When do you leave for New York? Her text read. I raised an eyebrow, surprised and flattered she'd been keeping up with my schedule.

On Tuesday, the day before the concert.

Morning or night? I frowned, unsure where this was going or even why she was texting me at all. I was very sure of my heart beating out of control, however, and it had nothing to do with my run.

Morning. Why? I answered, my head beginning to pound like it was in a band competition with my heart to see who could drum it out faster. A good twenty, thirty minutes went by with no response. But then the telltale three dots began to appear. I knew, because I'd sat down on a bench and stared at my phone the entire time.

My flight lands at six-fifteen tonight. I'll see you later.

I stared at the phone for a solid thirty seconds before sending a reply.

See me where? What flight? It was a stupid response. I should have known it would be greeted with—

My flight. To Nashville, obviously. I've got your address, so I'll just come there.

This is the part where I smiled. This is also the part where I wiped that smile off fast because she has a boyfriend and that's nothing to smile about, even if it is Jane, and she'd just announced she's coming here.

She's coming here.

I stood up and began to pace back and forth on the road.

Want me to pick you up? I'm not doing anything besides hanging out at the apartment.

No, I'll take a cab.

I shoved the phone in my pocket, because people look ridiculous staring at their phones while standing in the middle of the street, and I didn't want to be that guy. Even though I was wearing a baseball cap and the world's sweatiest, rattiest t-shirt, I'd get recognized just standing here, and I didn't want that either.

I ran back to my apartment in record time. It wasn't like Jane would be there already, but tell that to my legs. They were on a mission and who was I to make them slow down.

Besides, my apartment was a mess. Liam had left dishes all over the counter, and a few coffee grounds had missed the trash can and landed on the floor.

That was three hours ago. It's now two-thirty in the afternoon, and I'm standing in a spotless apartment since Sheila—the housekeeper—was willing to come right away. Judge me if you will, but I don't even own a vacuum, and I haven't scrubbed a toilet since the last time my mother grounded me. Might've been eighth grade. Maybe tenth.

I've looked at my Apple watch approximately one hundred million times in the past one-hundred eighty minutes. Jane is coming here tonight. This may be the worst possible idea in the history of ideas, but I won't pretend to be unhappy about it, at least not to myself. When Liam walks in the door and sees the excitement all over my face...that might be a little trickier to avoid. Especially because he'll call Chad and tell him, and when the two of them start giving me a hard time, it will last until Christmas, maybe longer.

I can't wait to see her. Seriously, can't wait. I'm so excited it's making me tired.

I think I'll take a nap.

CHAPTER SEVENTEEN

Jane

I'm not sure what the word *apartment* translates to in Teddy's mind, not now or when he used that word over text earlier, but this isn't it. In my world, an apartment consists of four hundred square feet of bedroom, bathroom, living room, and what barely passes for a kitchen. I have a tiny refrigerator and a two-burner stove with a microwave on an old moveable cart in the corner. My apartment is made up of plain white walls, linoleum flooring, and matted brown carpet that needed to be replaced two decades ago. But I can afford it, and it's in a safe enough neighborhood, so that's something.

By contrast, Teddy's apartment is designed around security gates and doormen and a speckled granite floor in the lobby. I stand at the elevator and stare at the lighted red numbers as they slowly fall to my level. The elevator stops on thirty-one and twenty-seven consecutively; I'll probably be here for a while. Which is just great, because time is what I need. There's nothing like using free time to second guess yourself.

What am I doing here?

I don't belong. I wore the wrong outfit. The Converse and ripped jeans and oversized black sweater don't fit with the well-heeled people milling in the lobby. This was a bad idea. I wish I'd been drinking when I booked the plane ticket; at least I'd have a muddled mind to blame and not a perfectly clear one.

I slide my hand across my silver monogrammed necklace a few times...thinking...talking myself out of actually riding this elevator to the thirty-ninth floor. The thirty-ninth. It practically screams penthouse. And that's when I decide. That's it. I'm done. Teddy's a big boy. He'll be fine. He has friends that can help him through this. What makes me think I—a practical stranger he spent a few hours with in a dark room over a week ago—can do anything? Looking at it from this angle, coming here was a ridiculous presumption on my part.

I turn on my rubber-soled heal to sneak away when someone familiar walks through the front door and spots me.

"Jane?"

I reluctantly smile at the tall guy from the night of the shooting, the one with the fiancé, both of whom were waiting for Teddy in the parking lot. Her name was...I don't remember. But she wants Teddy to wear a dress in her wedding. I remember that part. Teddy had a very large group of supporters. I remember that part, too.

"Hi?" I don't mean to say it like a question, but I can't remember the guy's name. Starts with an L or a D or something, I think.

He steps forward and holds out a hand. "It's Liam. I remember you from last week, not to mention everything Teddy's told us about you since. I didn't know you were coming."

"Neither did I." I smile weakly and shake his hand, suddenly self-conscious and feeling overwhelmingly foolish for showing up unannounced. I mean, Teddy knows I'm coming. But this guy is his roommate, and I've just barged my way into his life without asking permission. Maybe I should leave.

"Have you gone up yet, or did you just get here?" he asks.

I bite the inside of my cheek. I'm a professional body-guard but currently feel like a fourteen-year-old-girl afraid to walk into a school dance without a date.

"I got here ten minutes ago, but I'm a couple hours early. I caught an earlier flight and took a cab. Teddy gave me the address. I've been down here trying to work up the nerve to get on the elevator. Thirty-nine floors are a lot of floors."

He raises an eyebrow. "Afraid of heights?"

"Afraid of penthouses and famous country singers." I swallow. There's a strong possibility that was a bit too honest.

Liam laughs and pushes the button. "Don't worry, we're not nearly as fancy as this building." He reaches for my duffle bag, and I relinquish it. I packed light; my return flight is scheduled for two days from now, and I have a hotel reserved a few blocks away. Stopping here seemed like the logical first move, though I'm second-guessing that decision, along with my ability to make decisions in general. My judgment was way off. What am I doing here? "As for Teddy, I think he's more afraid of you than you realize." He winks, and all I can think is...

Afraid of me? There's no explaining the warmth that travels through me at the news, so I won't even try. He doesn't elaborate. I'm silently begging him to.

"Does Teddy know you're coming?"

"Yes, we texted about it earlier."

Liam scratches an eyebrow. From the small smile on his face, I suspect he's turning over this reality. "Sneaky sucker. He didn't even tell me. Probably knew I'd give him a hard time."

"Hard time?" *For what?*

Liam's smile breaks free at that; it's a nice one. "What do you say we go in there and give him a hard time together?"

I can't help but smile back. "We should probably go easy, or he may kick me out."

The elevator dings and the doors slide open. The thirty-ninth floor is even nicer than the lobby, if that's possible. The mahogany-paneled doors accented with bronze door knockers lining the hallway suggest it is. It's further proof that of all the elements in the world, I'm definitely out of mine.

"I can promise you, without a doubt, he will not kick you out."

I frown when he winks because there it is again. An inside joke that I'm standing just on the edge of. I feel like I should know what he means, but I'm clueless. Liam holds the door and motions for me to step through, then slides past me to lead the way. Three doors down, he pulls out a key and opens it.

When we step inside the apartment, I swallow a knot of discomfort before I remember why I'm here, and tell myself to get it together. Neither man is a stranger, and I know how to defend myself. Besides, Teddy needs help, and I'm here to give it. Enough with the public breakdowns. Enough with letting that gunman continue to terrorize our lives. Teddy has a concert tomorrow night. I'm going to see that he gets on stage to perform.

But when I round the corner and see him on the sofa, my optimism dissolves into a puddle at my feet. He's asleep, curled into one side of the sofa, his laptop in front of him. A video of his meltdown is paused on the screen, as though he'd been watching it and couldn't keep from reliving it. He's stuck in the lift, his eyes wide from fear. I know the part; I've watched it a dozen times myself. There's a newspaper on the floor, folded inside itself to an article about the shooting.

Forty-Nine-Year-Old Seattle Gunman Takes Five Lives And Injures Thirteen Others is the headline; underneath the article is a picture of Teddy, as though he and the shooter are one and the same. It's sloppy journalism at its worst, the reason so many no longer trust the media. If I were Teddy, I might be asleep too.

"Hey lazy, you have a visitor," Liam says, giving Teddy a shove on the arm as he passes down the hall. "I'll be in my room if you need anything." He says the words to me just before disappearing around a corner. Even from several feet away, I see the concern in his eyes. Joking over text is one thing, but witnessing someone in person is another. Teddy's more of a mess than I thought.

"Hey sleepy-head, I got here early," I say softly, lowering myself to sit next to his legs but careful not to touch them. Teddy startles at the sound of my voice and rolls onto his back, squinting up at me like he's unsure what he's seeing. He blinks and then seems to realize it, jolting upward to a sitting position.

"What time is it? Is it already seven?" His voice is thick like he's been asleep for a while. "I need to shower and change clothes before you get here."

I smile at his nonsensical words. "Well, I'm already here, so the window for that is closed. Want me to give you a minute? I could go pick up some dinner while you shower. I saw a little Italian place down the street."

Teddy reaches out a hand and I take it, swinging it between us a bit. He just stares at me, emotion making his breathing deep and his eyes heavy. I don't look away, convinced he's still waking up and doesn't know how much that look and his touch are affecting me. It's intense, like I'm a life raft thrown at him just before he drowns...like I'm a gallon jug of water after a five-mile run. Either that or the sight of me is making all the bad memories replay in his mind. Most likely a mix of everything.

Finally, he averts his gaze and takes a deep breath, rubbing his eyes with one hand.

"Food. Yes. Do you mind getting some? I swear I'll look better by the time you get back." He drops my hand and stands up, reaching for his wallet. He produces a credit card and holds it out to me.

I take it and raise an eyebrow. "You do realize I could still be a crazed fan that might use this on an outrageous shopping spree, right? Awfully trusting of you to just hand it over."

He flips his wallet onto the bar and stretches, working the kinks out after that nap. "You're not a crazed fan. Get me a pasta primavera, okay? And some Italian rolls, a Caesar salad, a few cannoli, and whatever you want."

"You'll eat all that?" I look him up and down. He's trim from head to toe, well built without an ounce of fat anywhere I can see. I hate men and their instant ability to convert calories into air.

"I'll probably eat some of yours, too." Again, with the wink. Again, with the warm feeling traveling up my spine. "Just a second though." He yells down the hall to Liam, asking for his order. It's loud and clear and even longer than Teddy's. "Did you get that?" he asks me.

"Um, I think I'll—"

"I'll text it to you. Are you sure you don't mind? Dillon is working tonight, so he'll be hanging with us for a while."

I smile. "I don't mind at all." It might ease some of the tension to have a third person here. Teddy takes a few steps away. I shoulder my purse and walk toward the door.

"Hey."

I stop and turn to find him standing right in front of me. Before I can ask what else he wants, he pulls me into a hug. His arms go around my waist and travel up my back, and I

can't help it. He smells the way I remember—woodsy and
expensive—but it's his hands that jumpstart my heart. They
briefly roam my back in circles, a move that's both intimate
and familiar. I lean in and hang on, and for the oddest second,
it feels like I've come home. That can't be right, can it? You
can't find a home in someone after a shared trauma. The
statistics are there. Those relationships never work. You can
find understanding, sure. Support, for certain. In some cases,
even friendship. But a home? Of course not.

"Thanks for showing up. You have no idea how much it
means."

He kisses me on the side of the head, and I feel myself
sink.

A home. You can't feel at home with one person when you
just broke up with another.

So why is this exactly the way I feel?

"Of course." I plant a kiss on his neck and peel myself
away. "I'll be right back."

I let myself out of the apartment and ride the elevator
back down again.

Sinking. Sinking.

Until I land on solid ground and the elevator doors open.

First things first, I head toward the restaurant. Italian
food, I'm on a mission to order it. Later, after I'm full and less
emotionally exhausted and thinking more clearly, then I can
deal with the way my life currently seems to be spinning out
of control.

I order all the pasta and bread and a slice of cheesecake
for myself.

Like I said, I'll deal with it later.

———

Teddy

I met my friend Chad in college. He rounded a corner outside the Science lab our freshman year and slammed right into me, knocking my books and the remainder of a Venti Starbucks triple shot white chocolate mocha onto the sidewalk. I wasn't fully awake and not in the best of moods, so I made some crack about his hillbilly haircut and told him to watch where he was going. Without missing a breath, he told me where I could shove my insult, called me a jackass, then picked up that Styrofoam cup and tossed it at me, sending flecks of brown liquid all over my new white Polo. I caught the cup upside down, giving the remaining coffee grounds a chance to slide down my arm. By the time I bent over to retrieve my books, Chad had walked away, leaving me alone with a stack of books I never planned to open and a killer headache that pounded between my ears.

Two things about that day stand out in my memory. One, Chad majored in finance, hailed from right here in Nashville, and was hardly a hillbilly—his second cousin was a somewhat known musician who sang back up for a locally popular performer who was gaining steam at the time. Plot spoiler: now she's a painter and probably makes more money than me on a one-hit-wonder that released a decade ago and is now used in a national insurance commercial. And two, I was, in fact, a jackass.

I ran into him—this time not literally—later that day in the cafeteria, shook his hand and apologized. We've been best friends ever since. Roommates for two years now, along with his brother Liam. Liam and I have grown close over the years, so close that both brothers are my best friends, the two people I've learned to count on more than anyone except for my cousin Dillon. Although, she wants me to be her maid of honor, so I'm not sure she's all that reliable anymore.

Right now though, as I see Liam's arm slung across the back of Jane's chair intently listening to her talk, I'm kind of jealous. If he wasn't engaged to Dillon, and hopelessly, sickeningly in love with her, I would probably hate him.

As it stands, I just want him to leave and—I don't know—go taste wedding cakes or something. Not grab another roll and...what the heck? Did he just take a bite of Jane's cheesecake? I've never been more envious of a fork. I keep shooting him death glares, none of which he's noticed because unlike the rest of the country, my friends are not affected by my presence. I'm not sure if Liam even remembers I'm here.

I'm aware all of this makes me seem like a diva, but my mental state isn't all that reliable now.

"And so you work at a bank part-time, but you work security at night? Is it a tough job?"

Jane offers Liam a weak smile. "Only if someone shows up with a gun." I flinch, which Liam sees. Funny how suddenly I don't want him to notice anything. "But other than that, my jobs are surprisingly uneventful."

"Except for almost getting shot," I mutter before thinking the better of it.

"But I didn't," Jane says, turning her focus me. "And neither did you."

I reach for my wine glass and take a sip, feeling two sets of eyes on me. Pasta sauce burns in my throat. The wine tastes fermented. Even my favorite cannoli has a bitter bite. Nothing feels right—not the conversation, not the forced pleasantries, not the lulls in both. It's so disturbing that I try to keep my eyes off Jane as much as possible even though she's the one person I want to talk to more than anything. It isn't easy, like trying to avoid gazing at a sunset or a rainbow. Everything within you wants to soak in the color and appreciate the beauty, but you know that if you stare too long, you'll never want to go inside again. That the walls of your own home will suddenly feel confining and suffocating. That nothing will seem right until you head back outside, enjoy the scenery, and breathe in the fresh air.

Jane is the scenery. Jane is the color. Jane is the air.

She stands up and gathers take-out containers, cleaning up the mess like she owns the place. I stare, still not entirely sure what made her come here. So many things I want Jane to clarify, but all I can do is sit still and watch the end of the night unfold. I stand to help her, and we make quick work of straightening up. It isn't long before her eyes grow tired, so I hug her goodbye. She hugs me back, then walks out to catch a cab, telling me she'll back in the morning, and once again refusing my offer to call for a driver.

There's a blazing fire in the fireplace, but my insides feel cold and clammy.

Liam leaves to see Dillon.

I hate being alone.

CHAPTER EIGHTEEN

Jane

By the time we pull into the parking lot late the next afternoon, he's onto me. Which is a combination of good and bad because at least one of us knows what we're doing. I booked the plane ticket, flew here, hopped in a cab, bought Italian food, ate dinner with two ridiculously handsome men. Consequently, I felt more intimidated than a girl in my profession should and slept on the world's lumpiest mattress last night, but that's where my inspiration stops. Now we're sitting in a parking lot, the faint pounding of a drumbeat off in the distance, and I'm lost for what to do next.

"Do you want to go in?" I ask.

"No."

His answer is so direct and final that I blink at the half-full lot, unsure what to do now. It's the same answer he's given all three times I've asked. This is where my whole plan begins and ends: me walking him into that arena and showing him how easy it would be. It's the whole reason I bought a plane ticket in the first place. Here. There. In. Out. Baby steps.

Baby steps. Done. Problem solved. Let's go get some ice cream.

Maybe I didn't think this through well enough.

"So, do you just want to sit here then?"

"Nope, but you're the driver, so it's not like I have much of a choice." He sulks and stares out the window while I look up at the billboard off to the left, a well-known pop singer staring back at me from thirty feet up. People begin to pull up and climb out of cars, most dressed in combat boots and ripped jeans to emulate the star of the show, but we stay put at Teddy's command. I'm completely lost for what to do. "I can't believe this is why you came to Nashville." He's angry. For the first time, I'm starting to feel that way too.

"I'm trying to help, Teddy. But it's your car, so actually, you do have a choice. If you want me to drive away, just say so." I'm behind the wheel of his Lexus because I insisted on driving even though the car is expensive, and getting behind the wheel made me nervous. But I knew he wouldn't come here if I told him where we were going, so I risked it. Inside the arena, a friend of mine is on the lookout, waiting for us to make an appearance. I'm now ninety-nine-point-nine percent sure we're not going inside, so I send the guy a quick text.

"What are you doing?"

"Texting my friend. Letting him know we're not coming. He's working security tonight, has worked here for years, so I'd texted him to see if we could get backstage and watch everything happen. I thought it might be good for you to see how things unfold as a spectator. Maybe it would take some of the pressure off you."

"That's just it, though. Spectators don't have any pressure, and it's those of us that headline who need to keep it that way. All these people are here for a good time. They don't know how quickly that good time can turn into a nightmare, because they've never experienced it. If there's no concert to attend, it will stay that way, and no one gets hurt. But here we are, charging all these people way too much money and putting them in danger while we do it."

His words picked up speed and volume as he spoke, like a politician at an election rally who has one last shot at swaying voters to their side. Everything Teddy just said is irrational, but he believes it so much that I almost believe it, too. I can see his point. If there's no show, there's no risk. It's the classic story of staying homebound to avoid all possibility of danger in the outside world. Sure, you're safe. But are you really living at all? Life without music is merely static and white noise. Life without adventure is simply existing. Like painting a rainbow in shades of gray and tan and cream. God doesn't make colorless promises, he doesn't want us to live muted lives, he doesn't want us to blend in with the clouds. He didn't breathe air inside our lungs just to leave us winded and weak.

I have no idea how to communicate that to Teddy when I'm sitting here just as scared as him. When I have been living that kind of muted life for more years than I want to admit.

"Maybe we should have stayed at your apartment tonight," I say.

"We should have," he agrees.

I nod and take a deep breath. "Maybe I should take you home, and maybe you should stay there for the rest of the year. You could order take-out for Thanksgiving and have a Christmas tree delivered. You could order all your presents off Amazon and hire someone to come wrap them. You could watch the ball drop at midnight and kiss your pillow Happy New Year. You could call your cousin and tell her someone else will need to be her maid of honor because you're unable to show up for her wedding, what with all the not leaving your house you have to do. You could do all these things, and then you will be safe. You'll also be incredibly disappointed and bored with life, but at least you'll be safe. Everyone else will be safe, too, because Teddy Hayes didn't show up with a target on his chest to put them directly in danger. Whew. What a relief that will be for everyone involved.

"What's your point?" he snaps.

I close my eyes for a second. "Just that you're being irrational." When I open my eyes again, I realize how dark it's getting and turn on the headlights. "But, hey, if you want to leave, we'll leave." I start the car and pull out of the parking space, my interest piqued when he cranes his neck to get a look at the fans pouring into the arena. They're coming in big groups now, chatting excitedly, a few singing off-key song lyrics, the concert only an hour away. Even from inside this car, the electric energy is palpable. Teddy lightly drums a finger on the console, the movement so faint he's likely unaware he's even doing it.

"Is this what people look like when they come to my shows?" The question is soft, timid, laced with an edge of surprise like it had never occurred to him fans would be so excited even before the show started.

"I remember the crowd being just like this, only there were more people because you're more popular. Lots of teenagers and mothers looking to have a good time."

He cringes, and I try not to smile. We're on a razor-thin corner of something I can't quite pinpoint, so I stay quiet. Silence seems like the best way to keep him from running... words may halt whatever wheel is turning in his mind. I turn left and pretend I couldn't care less. If this bodyguard gig doesn't pan out, I could always act for a living.

We're right next to the arena, so close you can feel the vibrations of the show gearing up inside as reverberations rattle the windshield and cup holder. Still, Teddy says nothing, so I keep driving. We make it maybe twenty more feet when he stops me.

"Wait."

I press the brake and accidentally jolt us to a stop.

"What's the matter?"

"Nothing. Just...stop here for a minute."

I slowly nod and pull over to the side. "Okay."

After a few seconds, he says, "Pull into a parking space."

"Okay," I say again, and find one a few feet away. I put the car in park and roll my window down, then turn the car off with the explanation, "I don't want to waste gas." Teddy buys it and leans back into the seat. So many people pass by on their way inside. Every so often, someone glances through the window—one girl even did a double-take at Teddy—but they all keep walking. It's hard to compete with the excitement surrounding a concert and the prospect of seeing someone you admire up close and in person. I felt that way when I saw Elton John for the first time. Yes, I'm a nerd, but I'm a nerd who knows good music.

"Mind if we stay here for a little while?" Teddy half-whispers, biting a thumbnail. "I want to watch."

This time my smile is hard to fight. It's getting darker outside, and people are getting harder to see, but the night air feels nice. It takes work, but I force my face and tone to remain neutral.

"I don't mind at all. I don't have any other plans."

Except I do...I did. This was my plan all along,

Baby steps.

Baby steps.

I just didn't think Teddy would go along with it.

The plan alters a bit when he reaches across the seat and threads his fingers through mine, bringing both our hands to his lap. Just like in the closet.

"Is this how you handled things after the baby?" he whispers. I freeze, hoping I heard him wrong and begging everything around me for an answer. Tonight isn't about me. It never has been, and I never want it to be.

"What do you mean?" My throat is tight and thick like someone inserted a fist and commanded me to talk around it.

"I mean after everything happened. Did it take you a while to start living again? How did you make it? How long did it take you to heal and move on?"

I clear my throat a couple times and answer softly. "I never did."

Teddy sits up abruptly. "I didn't mean...that sounded harsh. I wasn't trying to imply that it was something you should move on from. I don't imagine a person could ever get over that sort of pain."

I shake my head. He's misunderstood me. "No, it's okay. What I meant was, I haven't healed, even now. I realized it a few days ago. I've kept my life on pause all this time, thinking I deserved it. If she couldn't live, I couldn't either, you know?"

He sighs long and slow, sinking back into his seat. "You know that isn't true, right?"

"I do now."

We're whispering, just like we did in the closet. It's nice to know that with some people, you don't have to shout to be heard.

"I think you owe that to her, to live. It's what she would want for her mother." His words pierce my heart and eyes at the same time, and the tears rise and fall down my face.

"I think you might be right. It's taken me all these years to see it. I'm just not sure how to start."

He squeezes my hand a little tighter, a comfortable silence descending like a heated blanket, soft and welcome.

"Well then, maybe you came here as much for you as you did for me." He's right, another thing I'm just now seeing as well. "Want to sit here a while? Maybe we could start here."

I nod and settle into the seat, head back, eyes closed, thinking about ten years ago when I had my baby, thinking about last week when I broke up with Ben, thinking about now, as I sit here with Teddy and take one tiny baby step toward life.

Life throws a lot at you, and often the first instinct is to duck and run. But sometimes the best thing to do is sit still, turn to face it, let it speak to you, wait the chaos out, and trust that the process will make you stronger.

Baby steps.

Baby steps.

A plan put in motion for Teddy but suddenly meant for me.

―――――

Teddy

I'm holding her hand, but she hasn't pulled away, so I keep my fingers in place and tell myself not to overthink it. That's the thing about writers—about creatives in general—we overthink like it's a side job we don't get paid for, and telling ourselves to quit is about as productive as telling a mouse not to think about the cheese in front of his face. Pointless.

I don't know what it is about Jane, but she calms me in a way no one ever has. It isn't just trauma and tragedy, it's a sense that she knows me better than anyone, and showed up despite the fact. I'm confident, but not nearly as cocky as people think. They say image is everything, and I'm definitely one to feed the beast. But Jane sees through it and doesn't care. The last time a woman I just met didn't care if I acted like Teddy Hayes the Famous Country Singer or just Teddy the normal guy with real-life issues was...never.

Women want the superstar, no exceptions. I've heard this from everyone; I've experienced it firsthand for a few years now myself.

Jane is the exception.

"Is this really why you came here, to get me to an arena?"

Our hands rise and fall with her shrug. "It's one reason."

"What's another reason?"

"To get you *inside* an arena, not just to the parking lot. I'm beginning to think I flew all this way to catch pneumonia. It's getting cold in here."

I laugh at her honesty and reach behind me for a jacket I keep in the back seat. It's leather and was given to me by Brad Paisley when I opened for him two years ago, but I don't tell her that. Jane doesn't like country music anyway, so she wouldn't be that impressed. It's another reason I like her.

I look around. The parking lot is full, and almost no one is outside. The concert starts in two minutes, and I can hear the booming track of pre-set music warming up the crowd. In a handful of seconds, the music will stop, the crowd will scream, and the opening act will start.

Yep, there it is. The ear-piercing, teenage-girl heavy, screams. Pop, classic rock, or country, the crowd reaction is the same. There's nothing more powerful than a loyal, revved up fan base. Next to me, Jane smiles.

"I remember at your show...it was the first one I worked for that size. People were crazy with excitement. The screams almost made me crazy. What does that sound like when you're up on stage?"

I stare straight ahead for a moment, trying to put it into words. "It sounds like affirmation and adrenaline being thrown at you all at once. Hearing the crowd collectively scream your name is a rush. It makes you want to perform better, present better, be better. It's a bit of a crash every night after it's over, though. Whiplash without the car wreck."

She laughs. "I'll bet. No one's ever screamed my name

unless I was late for curfew or spilling cereal all over the floor."

I can think of a couple other instances where someone might scream her name, but I keep it to myself and shift in place, suddenly even more aware of her hand on my thigh. "Bit of a problem child, were you?"

"You can say that. Definitely by the teen years."

I don't miss the way her smile fades or the sadness behind her words. All roads point back to whatever you endured in your youth, don't they? No matter how much life you live, you can never quite shake them. I guess they aren't called the formative years for nothing. I give her hand a squeeze and lean my head back, actually enjoying the night despite my uneasiness at the location.

"There's something we have in common, I suppose. My teen years sucked, too."

She rolls her head to the side to look at me. "How so? Other than being too small for football." She smiles, but I don't.

I tell her everything. About the torture, about the bullies, about being locked all night in the locker room. The words come out in a rush so I don't have time to overthink them. It's only after I'm finished talking that I realize I've never shared the story with anyone but Dillon. I suppose until now, I've never trusted anyone enough to keep it to themselves.

"You're right, teenage years suck." She takes a deep breath. "Is that why you became a musician? To prove the bullies wrong?"

I look out the window. "No, I became a musician because I had a lot of time to myself back then. When you don't have any friends, you make friends with things that speak in other ways. My guitar became my sidekick. After a while, we added my voice to the mix and developed a pretty good team."

She laughs. "It appears that way. The three of you have definitely made something of yourselves."

"We're not doing too bad."

I smile at the silly conversation, then laugh outright when she says, "so how many of those awful kids from school have asked for tickets to a show?"

"All of them."

Her eyes narrow. "I hope you told them no."

You would think that, wouldn't you? "Nope. I've put them all on the front row. And when they reach up to shake my hand, I pass them over. Sometimes it's more fun to get revenge without saying a word. And it gives me a pretty good view to see their reactions."

She laughs. "I wish I could see that."

"Maybe someday you will."

The weight of the words I've spoken settles heavy because they imply I'll be back onstage at some point. Maybe I will, but for now, I'm not ready.

"Mind if we stay here a while longer?"

"We can stay here until the show is over if you want to." Her words have a ring to them, an outline that sounds a little like hope. I can't deny the suggestion sounds appealing. I saw the crowd walk into the building; it might be nice to see them come back out.

"Let's just hang here for a bit, and we'll leave when we get tired of it."

"Okay." Jane sighs like she's tired and settles into the seat. Unable to help myself, I pull her hand up to mouth and plant a light kiss on her knuckles.

"What was that for?" she whispers.

"For being here. For trying to help."

"I'll stay as long as you want," she says. Then she turns her head away from me. I can't decide if she's staring out the window or just doesn't want me to read her expression. It could be a little of both.

We stay until the end of the show, watching as people file excitedly out of the building.

Unharmed.

We stay another hour after that.

I'm fully aware Jane is giving me time to process what it all means. It works. Somehow, it works.

"Can you ask your friend if we can come to tomorrow night's show?"

From the look on her face, I think I've done something good.

CHAPTER NINETEEN

Jane

I call my friend Rick the next morning to let him know we're coming, then spend the next hour alternately rummaging through the meager contents of my bag and cursing my utter lack of packing skills. No matter how many times I pull everything out, the outcome stays the same: I brought one pair of jeans, a pair of yoga pants, a sweatshirt and a sweater. There's not a cute dress anywhere in sight, not one single outfit that conveys I'm Going To Save My Friend's Career And Also Make Him Think I'm Cute. Not one. No one looks good in yoga pants unless they're an actual yoga instructor or Cindy Crawford's daughter, and I'm not either one. I'm more like Cindy Crawford's part-time chef, complete with a ketchup stain on my sweatshirt. I ate hashbrowns this morning at the free breakfast buffet, but that isn't the point. The point is there's one less option for me to wear tonight because I packed stupid outfits.

I'm going shopping.

"Can you ask your friend?"

I still can't believe he said that; can't believe something I planned actually sort of maybe worked. So much could still go wrong tonight. A loud noise might set him back, a fan could get hurt in some way that has nothing to do with outside influence, the show could be bad. I've never heard of the band performing, but apparently, they're popular in certain underground circles. Still, it's a sold-out show, so I suppose that means something. But Teddy's on the brink here; I may inflict physical harm to anyone who threatens his progress. Maybe not the best attitude under the circumstances, but it's real. My phone rings from inside my bag. It takes a minute to locate it under all the loose change and—hey!—a flattened Milky Way chocolate bar I didn't know I had. But I find it and answer. I peel back the wrapper and take a bite.

"Hello?" My mouth is full, and it's obvious to whoever is calling.

"What are you eating?" It's Rick calling, and he sounds grossed out.

"A Milky Way."

"You shouldn't be eating that garbage," he says. "Also, I need you to bring Teddy around to the back entrance, side door B, okay? It's the loading door, so there will be vans and trucks, it should be easy to see."

I take a sip of water and swallow. "Okay, we'll be there."

"Good. Try to get there an hour early so we can get through security. It might take a bit longer tonight, so we want to be safe."

I frown. "Why tonight? Is something wrong?"

"No, we're just being extra cautious since the incident at Teddy's concert. Everyone is. And this crowd...they aren't known for being the calm, passive type." Rick laughs a little. I don't at all. Suddenly, I'm second-guessing everything.

"What do you mean? They're violent?"

"No, not violent. Just usually a little drunk. Maybe strung out on one thing or another."

I press a hand to my forehead and sink onto the bed. "Rick, I can't bring him to a show with a bunch of half-crazed, stoned fans who need extra security. What if something happens?"

"Nothing's going to happen, trust me. Just get there early, alright? I'll take care of you. Just be prepared for this crowd. I doubt it's like one you've ever seen before." Again with the laugh. It's tinny and high-pitched and perfectly matches the cold, pointy witch's finger running down my spine. *My pretties. I saved an apple just for you.*

What have I gotten us into?

"Okay," I say, "I'll trust you, but don't let me down."

"I'm getting you in the doors, aren't I? I won't let you down." He hangs up, and I fall backward, worried about much more than my outfit now.

Nothing about his words makes me feel better.

———

I turn in the full-length mirror, questioning the way I look in my black ripped jeans, leather vest, and boots, but it's the eyeliner that really has me pausing at this newfound sense of deviant style. I've never worn this much eyeliner in my life, but the make-up artist at Sephora assured me it looked "hot"—his words, not mine. My hair was curled with a spirally-wand-thingy by the girl working one chair over, a veritable one-stop-shop-and-makeover just waiting to happen. Who knew mall beauty stores could be that efficient? Certainly not me, possibly because I hate to shop. I especially hate mall beauty stores.

On any other day, I consider a mall to be one of the many branches of hell. Others include nail salons, bid day on college campuses, Black Friday sales, any photoshoot that involves cheerleader poses or duck lips, and the hymn *I'll Fly*

Away, which should obviously not be considered a part of hell whatsoever because it is a song about Jesus. But to me, it is. In my defense, if it wasn't for the old man I sat behind every Sunday who stood up and flapped his hands like a bird every time the organ played that song all those years ago in church, I wouldn't consider it hellish at all. The man scared me to death with those dance moves every week, so the song is on my list. Apologies to the writer of what otherwise might be a beautiful hymn, who is most certainly penning more glorious hymns in heaven as we speak.

Anyway, my outfit. I'm not sure I should—

A knock on my hotel room door ceases all thoughts of my attire. Doesn't matter anyway, I'm out of time now.

Looking longingly at my ketchup-stained sweatshirt and leggings left in a heap on the floor, I walk to the door and open it, smiling wide at Teddy to let him know I am not afraid, we are in this together, I will not leave his side, and I will help him heal.

He doesn't smile back, just looks at me and frowns.

"What the heck are you wearing?" he asks. My left arm tugs on a lightning-bolt earring as I give myself a once-over and then take him in. That's when I notice the small but very real difference in our fashion choices.

He's wearing black jeans, a matching black sweater, and sneakers. We both went for the same color, but he managed to make it a thousand percent more comfortable. And he looks exceptionally hot.

"There's nothing wrong with what I'm wearing. Don't you think you should have dressed more appropriately? Their music is pretty hardcore, and the lead singer wears more eyeliner than I'm currently wearing. I looked him up on Wikipedia."

"It looks incredible, by the way. Yours, not his."

I smile. "Thanks."

"I'm just not sure how I feel about the chain."

My smile drops, and I glance down. There's indeed a chain running from my vest to a belt loop, but I thought maybe it gave me a badassery vibe I was otherwise lacking. Clearly, I was wrong. I unhook the chain and fling it toward the bed.

"There. Better?"

"A matter of opinion. Though if you'd answered the door holding a whip in your hand, I might have suggested we stay in tonight." He grins. My face flames red and threatens to melt off the carefully-applied eyeliner. I clear my throat with difficulty.

"I'll ignore that comment." No, I won't. I'll be thinking about it this time next year. "Are you ready to go?"

"Your chariot awaits. Sadly, all I brought was my car. Hope you and your biker-chick vibe aren't too disappointed I don't own a motorcycle." He eyes my outfit again, then pushes the elevator button, and we step inside.

"Shut up, Teddy." My face is still warm, and I'm fighting a smile.

"I still think it's a shame you didn't buy a whip," he quips. I roll my eyes as we step off the elevator.

"If I had, I'd just use it on you." It was meant to be a threat. That isn't how he takes it.

"Baby, this isn't the time to give me that mental image. Maybe later, after the show." He laughs at his little joke and opens the car door for me.

I want to tell him to shut up again, but funny...I can't seem to speak. When he closes the door and walks around to the driver's side, I quickly blow on my face, trying frantically to cool it off.

———

Teddy

All jokes aside, by the time we pull up to the arena, I'm back to being terrified. A cold sweat has broken out on my upper lip, and my back feels clammy and uncomfortable. My hands shake, same with my legs. When Jane asks if I'm ready to go, I want to scream, "No."

Instead, we climb out of the car. I'm not sure how she feels about me reaching for her hand, but I don't ask, and it's too late for formalities anyway. With her, it's just what I do. I can't be next to her without connecting physically; it's been that way from the literal first second we met and will continue to be unless she changes things. I won't, because Jane is my person.

Can someone be your person when you don't even know their middle name? That's weird, isn't it?

"What's your middle name?" I ask without giving it a second thought. With some things, you don't think twice, much like that kiss I gave her in the closet. I need to know her full name almost as much as I wish I could kiss her. Honestly, I can't kiss her again until I know it, because in light of everything we've been through, that just seems weird. And she has a boyfriend, so thoughts of kissing her need to get out of my brain ASAP.

"Jane," she says. I frown.

"Jane's your middle name?"

"Yes. My first name is Allison. So basically, I have two awful names, and my parents decided to call me the least bad of the two."

"Your names aren't bad at all."

"Tell that to the kid called either Allison Smellyson or Plain Jane all through school. Not to mention G.I. Jane, by every other person who heard my name in passing."

"Smellyson? Kids really need to work on their insults. But I take exception with G.I. Jane. She's a badass. Every boy in

America thinks so, and all those boys turn into grown men who—I promise—think of G.I. Jane the second you say your name."

"Like you did in the closet?"

I smile, busted. "Like I did in the closet. But in my defense, it was completely dark, so I had to rely on my imagination. You had a gun on your hip at first, and of course, I filled in the blank with black pants, combat boots, and the required vest. But I'll admit, in my version, you had a buzz cut, bulging biceps, and a few tattoos."

She laughs, and it sounds like music. I love her laugh. "Sorry to disappoint."

"Hardly a disappointment. When the lights came on, I couldn't believe what I was seeing. Ben is a lucky guy."

We approach the back door, and she knocks. "Ben is also a thing of the past." She says it so quietly I almost don't hear her. But I do. In fact, I hear her words so loudly they almost don't register until we walk inside, shake a few hands, and get ushered to the band's dressing room.

Jane and Ben broke up?

Good. That guy was a jerk.

But...now she's free. Right? For a guy who should be nervous to be in this arena, Jane's words are all I can think about. She's single. She's single and she's here.

That thought—more than anything else—is what gets me through the next hour.

CHAPTER TWENTY

Jane

I've kept my eye on Teddy throughout the entire show, watching for signs of panic or distress, but I haven't seen anything of note since the single incident at the beginning; two if you count the flinch.

When the lights first went off, he jerked backward and took my hand with him. It didn't hurt, but it took him a second to calm down. After a breath or two, he settled into place next to me again, his side pressed to mine, and his hand clenching mine like it was a lifeline he might accidentally sever. His breathing remained tight and shallow, but he was okay. After a moment, he was okay.

But then the first set of fireworks went up, and he turned and walked away. We were standing off to the side of the stage where no one could see, so he had room to pace. Which he did, back and forth with his hands behind his head as I stood beside him and watched. It's hard to see someone you care about melt down in front of you, but I stayed. I had to. When you really care about someone, you endure the good times and the ugly; you don't leave when they need you most. Teddy needed me, and I wasn't going anywhere.

"I can't watch, I can't watch," he kept muttering to himself. But he did. It took a bit longer this time, but he came back to the edge of the stage and didn't leave for the rest of the show. A few minutes into it, he began to relax. Halfway through the first set, I caught him singing along, surprised to find he knew every word to the songs. Teddy is country...or so I thought? Grunge doesn't seem like his scene, but maybe I don't know enough about him. A theory tested when toward the end, he began dancing in place. Let me tell you, the sight of Teddy Hayes dancing is something I won't soon forget. Sexy doesn't even begin to describe it. I'll probably dream about it tonight. I'll probably still be dreaming about it when I'm eighty, and I've lost all memories except this one.

The concert ended ten minutes ago, and we've been hanging out with the band backstage since then. And you know how the experts say not to assume you know people by what you see online? It's a lesson we should all probably adhere to. How do I know this?

Because right now, as we speak, I'm watching a man with black spikey hair, gauges in both ears, an especially painful-looking lip ring, and two arms covered in tattoos that make me want to cry for all the hours he must have spent getting prodded with a needle...change a baby's diaper while making cooing noises in her face. Every time he comes close, she kicks and babbles excitedly, and I feel a bit more put in place for my pre-conceived notions.

"How old is she?" Teddy asks him—the guy's name is Steve, by the way. Not Viper or Stone or Jagger or any other array of dangerous names I could have come up with. Just Steve. Plain and simple like the long-ago star of Blue's Clues, except his sidekick is an adorable newborn.

"Three months. She's got Daddy wrapped around her

pinky toe, don't you sweet thing?" *Pinky toe?* I marvel when he picks her up and plants a succession of kisses up and down her neck. She squeals in delight, and my ovaries do a few somersaults inside my body.

"Can I hold her?" Teddy asks, sending those same ovaries tumbling down a hill and straight into a tree.

"Sure man, just remember to hold up her head a bit like this." Viper slash Steve demonstrates while Teddy settles her into his arms. I look away to compose myself, overwhelmed by the sight of these two larger-than-life men fawning over someone so cute and tiny.

"You look like a natural, Teddy." A woman who looks like a life-sized Teresa doll—you know, Barbie's best friend—comes in from the other room and wraps Viper in a hug. Sorry, I just can't think of him as a Steve. "That was a great show, Babe. One of the best I've seen." She links her hands around his waist and smiles big, and then she spots me.

"I'm sorry, I don't think we've met. I'm Sarah, Steve's wife. Are you a friend of Teddy's?"

Steve and Sarah? What is this world I've walked into?

"Yes, I'm Jane, Teddy's body—"

"Friend," Teddy speaks up. "She's my friend. Flew in from Seattle a couple nights ago."

I nod, my mouth suddenly dry at his use of the word *friend*. I assumed he saw me as his bodyguard and nothing more. I guess I was wrong, something that's increasingly clear tonight.

"It was a great show," I say. "Thanks for letting us be here. Teddy knows all the words to your songs, just so you know." I laugh, as does everyone else. But for a different reason, I quickly learn.

"He should. He helped write three of them," Viper says. "Been a few years, but it's good to know you remember them."

My mouth falls open, because...Teddy wrote those songs? I thought he only knew how to write about beer and heartbreak. He sees the look on my face and laughs.

"I think you just shocked the heck out of my date. What —did you think I only knew how to write about beer and heartbreak?"

"Um..." it's all I can manage to say, and everyone laughs except me. I'm still stuck on the word *date*. Just who is taking care of whom tonight? Because I can tell you for sure that I'm completely incapable of being much use to anyone right now. "Can I hold the baby?" I ask, more out of desperation than anything else. I need something to do with my hands so no one can see them shake. I need something to think about besides liking the sound of that word.

Teddy hands her off, and I bury my face in hers. Man, babies smell good. The distraction works so well that I soon forget what had me so flustered. She smiles at me, and I smile back. Soon it becomes a game of who can make the most ridiculous noises. I become so absorbed in the baby that I barely hear Viper say, "Watch out Teddy, soon she'll be wanting one, and you'll find yourself as whipped as me."

I also barely notice the way Teddy doesn't respond, just grins softly at me like he knows something I don't.

———

Teddy

We're halfway back to the hotel when I think of it, the perfect way to describe everything I've felt the past two weeks, from fear to anxiety to paranoia to extreme gratefulness. I don't voice it, though. I can't. Maybe later, after I've had time to think.

"Thank you for coming with me tonight. It helped." I would reach for her hand, but I'm already holding it. It occurs to me then that I've never asked if it bothers her. "Do you mind that I'm always grabbing your hand? I hope it's not too forward, it's just that—"

"No, I don't," she says, squeezing once before looking out the passenger window. "At this point, I might think something was wrong if you didn't." She sighs, long and slow. "It's a bit surreal, though, if I really let myself think about it."

"What is?"

"The idea that Teddy Hayes is holding my hand. It's definitely not something I would have thought possible this time last month."

"Then don't think about it. I am just a guy, you know. A lot like Steve and the guys back there. I'm a guy who likes music and figured out a way to make money doing it, same as them."

She breathes a laugh. "I still can't believe you wrote some of those songs. They were screaming in a couple of them."

"What can I say, I'm a man of many hidden talents." I don't miss the way her face reddens, which was my goal in making that comment in the first place. Score one for me.

"Who would have thought a country musician could write like that."

"Still not a fan of country, are you?"

"Nope." She shakes her head, and I try not to feel disappointed. Lucky for me her phone lights up with an incoming text, highlighting her screen. It isn't the text I find interesting, however. It's her temporary screen saver.

"Then what is that?" I try to reach for the phone, but she jerks it away in a lightning-quick jolt.

"Nothing," she says, but her face is as red as my grandmother's tomato plants.

"That's not nothing. Show me your phone."

"I don't have to."

"Show me your phone, or I'll pull the car over."

"Pull the car over, and what? Make me walk back to the hotel?"

No, of course, I won't. "Yes, of course, I will."

She gives me a long, impatient look. And then hands it over. And sweet Mary and Joseph, I'm looking at her Spotify account. And on her Spotify account, there's a song pulled up. And on the song cover, there's a big fat picture of me. For some people, winning the lottery or inheriting a large sum of money might be the best day of their lives.

This just might be mine.

"You're listening to my songs." It isn't a question.

"No, I'm not."

"Then how do you explain this?" I shove her phone in her face, giving her a close-up of the Spotify screen saver.

"So what if I'm listening to your songs? It just means that —" she stops there, working on a retort but clearly having no luck.

"You like my music?"

She presses her lips together before opening them in a dramatic sigh. "Fine, maybe it's growing on me."

The loud *whoop* I make might be a bit obnoxious, but hearing Jane's laughter makes it worth it. I hand her back the phone as we pull into the hotel parking lot, and I maneuver into a space. For a man so good with words, I have no idea how to end this. It's been a surprisingly great evening, one I'm not sure we'll ever repeat.

"Well, I'm off to New York in the morning. It's a long drive, so we're leaving early."

"How are you feeling about it? Do you think you'll be able to perform?"

I sigh because I honestly don't know. "I'll try. That's about as good as I can promise right now."

She nods wordlessly, her throat constricting on a swallow. It's one of those movements a person makes when they don't know what to say, or when they have so much to say they aren't sure where to start.

Where she starts, however, sets me back a few steps.

"Do you want me to come with you?"

I blink in surprise, my chest vibrating as my heart beats against it violently. "To New York?"

"I mean, I don't have to. Just if you need me to. If you think it will help. I still have three days off work, but—"

"Yes." Sometimes you leap for what you want and think about it later. This is one of those times. "If you have time and don't mind, I would love the company."

"I don't mind." She searches my face, looking for an answer that neither of us can find yet.

"So...you broke up with Ben?" The timing of my question is odd, but it seems more important than anything.

"Yes." she nods. "A few days ago. It was time. Past time, actually. I realized I need to make some changes. They've been long overdue."

I nod and slide my hands up and down the steering wheel, then shift in place.

"Maybe you can tell me about them on the bus." I take a deep breath to keep myself from begging. "Okay, I'll pick you up at nine the morning. You're sure?"

"More than sure," she whispers, reaching for the door handle. "I'll be ready."

"Wait," I blurt before she steps out of the car. Without second-guessing myself, I reach for her hand and pull her toward me, embracing her across the seat, sliding as close as I can to her with the console between us. When hugging isn't enough, I kiss her on the forehead and hug her again. "Thank you so much for coming. You have no idea..."

She doesn't, because I haven't found a way to communicate it to her.

Yet.

"You're welcome." I feel her smile against my neck just before she pulls back and greets me with that smile face to face. She reaches up to push my hair off my forehead, and damn if it isn't the sexiest thing I've ever experienced. Playfully, she lets it fall into my face and tugs on a strand.

"I'll see you at nine."

"See you at nine."

I watch her walk inside before I pull out of the lot.

I need to pack.

And then I need to give a voice to the idea that latched on a few hours ago and hasn't let go since. The worst part: I only have tonight to do it.

CHAPTER TWENTY-ONE

Jane

I barely paid attention to Teddy's concert a few weeks ago, too focused on staying in position and checking my surrounding area for anything suspicious. Clearly, I should have been more thorough, something I've thought about approximately every few seconds or so since we walked out of that arena in Seattle. True, the shooter didn't originate from my particular area, but the fact that he made it inside at all is at least a partial failure on my part. Tonight I'm on the lookout even though I'm not on the clock. Habits don't change just because circumstances do.

Or venues.

Madison Square Garden is more than a little intimidating. Teddy attempting to tackle his fear at this particular arena has me more than slightly worried, mostly because this place is overwhelming in size and number. I peek out at the growing crowd once again, something I've done three times in the last ten minutes. I'm nervous, not for Teddy's safety, but for his state of mind. Despite the unfortunate outcome of his last few shows, this place is sold out and quickly filling up.

Forty thousand spectators all here for him. Even I feel nauseous at that number, and I have nothing to do but listen.

The opening act—a fifteen-year-old up-and-comer people are speculating might be the next Taylor Swift—has already taken the stage. She's pretty good, if you like country music, cowboy boots, and songs about heartbreak, which I do not despite what Teddy saw on my phone a couple days ago. I mean, I might slightly enjoy a song or two of his, but that's it. Maybe three, tops. I have had one stuck in my head all after-noon. I knock on the door and open it slowly, just in case he's not quite ready.

"Come in," he says, and it's all the permission I need.

"It's almost full out there. How are you doing?" I step inside his dressing room, trying to be encouraging while attempting to act like the professional I am. It's a front; inside, I'm jittery and nervous that things won't end well. That feeling that took root when I glanced at the crowd now multiplies when I see him sitting in a chair across the room. His elbows rest on his knees, his hands clenched together in a kneading fist, his head bowed low in what looks like prayer. He might actually be praying—who knows?—but I would feel better about it if anxiety didn't waft up and outward from his shoulders like the grim reaper rising from a nap.

"Not great," he says without looking up. "I keep thinking about the gunman, about the girl he shot before I even knew what was happening. I thought a firework malfunctioned." He looks up. "Did you know that? A firework, so I kept singing on the lift, thinking someone else would check on it. I remember it rising and then being lowered, and for a second, I was annoyed. I thought someone was screwing up the routine, and I was angry because I thought it might make me look unprofessional. Someone lay bleeding on the floor, and I was worried about my image. It was the main thing on my mind until you grabbed me."

"Teddy, there was no way you could have known."

"That's just it. I didn't know because I was too self-absorbed to know. The only thing I was thinking about was how bad that one mistake made me look. As if a lowering crane mattered more than anything else. Who does that? What kind of person thinks of himself more than anyone else at the same time people around him are getting shot? Fame changes you, and not in a good way..."

I kneel in front of him and reach for his hands. "Stop. Everyone does this, not just famous people. I was there, remember? Fireworks were going off, and everyone was screaming your name. It was so *loud*. You had no way of knowing anything was amiss. At the very beginning, I didn't know it, and it's my job to know. So what, you're self-absorbed sometimes. But so is everyone else."

The look in his eye changes from canceling shows? To punish yourself?" He shrugs, and my insides collapse with the knowledge. "Don't do that, Teddy. Don't walk off tonight because you think you need to be punished for what happened in Seattle. You don't. You've punished yourself enough."

"Other people were punished more. Some permanently."

"First of all, people buy tickets to concerts all the time, Teddy. They go to movies and grocery stores and churches and schools, never thinking today might be the day they get gunned down. As far as punishment goes, you didn't punish anyone. You were doing your best to entertain them...to give them two hours to have a good time and not think about whatever problems were going on in their lives. It's called talent Teddy, not ego."

I take a deep breath to calm myself down. When I get passionate about things, sometimes I can get carried away. Now isn't the time to get carried away.

"The shooter hurt those people, not you. He deserves to

be punished, you don't. So the way I see it is this: You can let those shots he fired in Seattle be the end of your career, or you can march out there on stage, pick up a microphone, and fire a proverbial last shot at the crowd in the form of your music. Gunmen like to put fear in people, Teddy; don't let him do that to you. All these people showed up tonight to hear you sing, so give them what they came for. Starting tonight, let the last shot and the first shot and all the in-between shots be yours, not his. Move your life and career forward on your terms. Don't make any decisions based on his."

He stares at me wide-eyed, which makes me think I may have gotten a little passionate there at the end. But I meant every word. It's happening more and more, people cowering to other people's wrath. Other people's judgment. Other people's awful, awful decisions. God didn't put us on this earth to live in fear of the next *what if*, but it seems like that's what people are doing more and more these days.

Haven't I spent the last decade doing the same thing myself?

I'm tired of it.

It's time we all stand up and begin to take our lives back.

This is what I'm thinking when I realize I'm still staring at him.

"You should be a motivational speaker, did anyone ever tell you that?" He slowly grins, and I win the billion-dollar lottery.

I smile back and bite my lip. "Only everyone I know. Get out there on stage, and I'll consider it."

He sits another minute just staring at me, that grin on his face that I can't quite read. It's funny, Teddy in the darkness is easier to decipher than Teddy in the daylight. I'll have to work on it.

"What?" I say when I can't take it any longer. Having a

superstar grin at you isn't an easy thing to handle even if you don't much like his particular brand of stardom.

Which I don't.

For some reason, I have to keep reminding myself of this.

He reaches up and chucks me on the chin, and my teeth tap lightly together. "I'm just glad you pulled me into that closet. You saved my life, maybe in more ways than one." He slides forward, cups my face in his hands, and kisses me on the forehead.

Is there any more romantic kiss than that?

I don't think there is.

"Still no boyfriend, huh?" he half-whispers, his voice husky and thick.

I press my lips together and work at keeping my composure. "Nope. We're broken up for good."

He stands up and stretches, then rolls his head a couple times before looking back at me with a wink. "Good, because after this show I'm going to kiss you for real. Be ready for it."

I watch as he pulls his phone from his pocket and sets it on the dressing table, reaches for a water bottle, and walks out of the room without looking back. A good thing, because I'm still staring with a lovesick grin that makes even me nauseous.

He's only a couple steps out of the room when he yells. "Go stand at the edge of the stage and watch! I'll be looking for you!"

"Okay!" I yell back, then turn to grab my own water, pausing when his phone lights up on the glass table in front of me. Unable to resist, I look down at the screen. It's an incoming text from his cousin Dillon.

Fine, forget the purple dress. But if you don't call me back after the show and give me an update, then I'll make you wear a purple suit, got it? *Purple? What happened to red?*

I laugh, then walk out of the room to join Teddy stage-side. Sure, I'm excited to see him perform. But right now, more than anything else, I really hope he invites me to this very bizarre wedding.

Something tells me seeing Teddy in purple might be even better than seeing him dance.

———

Teddy

Fear is my enemy as I tuck myself onto the lift that will carry me up to the stage, just like that night two weeks ago. Fourteen days can pass in a blur or alter the trajectory of your life, depending on what happens in the span of those three-hundred hours. In my case, it's changed everything. I've aged a decade and grown weary with anxiety and developed a new life-plan. From now on, I'm in control—aside from God, of course. With His help, starting now, I say how I perform and what to be worried about and whether fear gets to have a say in any of it.

I've also developed a new philosophy: no matter what happens, I have the last word. Not some crazed shooter who was hell-bent on wreaking havoc on me and everyone in that Seattle arena. Not even the fans with their wavering level of support. Me, and only me.

And also maybe a knock-out blonde chick currently waiting in the wings, who gifted me with that philosophy only a few short minutes ago. She might run a couple things too one day.

The lift stops in front of me, and adrenaline rushes through my bloodstream, fear mixing in to make things interesting. Am I afraid? Of course, I'm afraid. Am I worried when the lights blind me, and I can't see danger if it strikes again tonight? Of course, I'm worried. Do I flinch when the fireworks blast and opening drumbeats multiply? Of course, I flinch. Do I hesitate when the lift door opens, and it's time to step inside? Of course, I hesitate. Do I remember that night two weeks ago when it lowered, and a woman grabbed me from behind and pulled me over the side? Of course, I remember.

Once I'm in, I turn around to look at her. I smile, thrilled at the way she smiles back. She's safe, and so am I. And she was right: facing a fear makes that fear smaller. It grew in my mind, and now I'm watching it shrivel. It won't go away completely, but it will fade. Time always heals what wounds try to destroy, this is no exception. I'm sure of it. Of course, I'm sure about something else, too.

I am going to kiss Jane later, so hard she'll never forget it.

On the ascent, I look out over the crowd and suck in a breath. I knew this place was big, but nothing prepared me for this view. They're all looking up, watching the lift take me higher and higher just like it's supposed to. I told the band I had a new song, so they wait for me to play. When I begin, I sing the song I penned on the bus. I sing it loud, alone, because the band hasn't heard it before. *Ninety Minutes in November* is the title. I sing it for Jane. I sing it for every minute of the night we spent in the closet. I sing it for the night that changed my life. I look down to see her wiping her eyes. And all I can think about is one single thing:

I'm performing at freaking Madison Square Garden, and forty thousand people are listening to every word. Even better, the girl I care about more than everyone combined is hearing them with tears in her eyes and a smile on her face. The moment is nearly perfect.

No one can take that away from me.

———

I find her walking out of the bathroom backstage. She's looking down, drying her hands on her jeans, so she doesn't notice my approach. I'm dripping with sweat and tired as I've ever been, but I'm on an adrenaline high that won't come down anytime soon, because I did it.

I freaking did it.

I was scared out of my mind until mid-way through the second set, but I don't think anyone noticed. I pushed through raging fear, kept singing, and fired that shot just like Jane told me I should. It's all thanks to her. If she hadn't come with me...if she hadn't delivered that pep talk before I stepped on stage...I'd probably still be sitting in that chair with my head between my knees. I owe her everything.

Jane.

She still hasn't looked up. She doesn't need to.

I hook her by the belt loop and pull her into me, crashing my mouth to hers like I've wanted to since I stepped on stage. Hell, since I first kissed her in the closet two weeks ago. At first, she's surprised, stills for a moment as though trying to comprehend who's kissing her in the first place. Of course, it's me. And it's time she knows it.

I kiss her harder and push her backward a few steps until we're back inside the bathroom, then use a foot to close the door behind us. The whole world keeps me under their scrutiny, but this moment is private. Prying eyes, look away. This might get a little R-rated.

Okay, PG-13. I'm not a monster.

I back her against the door and press into her, threading my hands through her hair, trembling at the way her fingers dance up my spine. I could get high on her touch alone, might just try it for the rest of my life.

The rest of my life.

It comes as a shock to my subconscious, but the thought isn't an unwelcome one.

I keep kissing her, thinking about the possibility. I get lost in it. So lost that it startles me when she pulls back and forces me out of my thoughts.

"What was that for?" she asks, a smile in her voice and in her eyes.

I keep a hand behind her neck, the other gripping her waist. I'll answer her question, but then we'll get back to where we were.

"For being here. For making tonight possible. For being you."

Her smile grows wider and more flirtatious. "Good answer."

"Mind if I keep doing it for a while?" I feel myself grin. I can take no for an answer, but I really don't want to.

"Not at all." Another good answer; we're both full of them tonight.

"Good."

The time for talking is over.

I'm back to kissing Jane. Even as people start to call my name. Even as footsteps mill around outside. Even as someone knocks on the door and yells, *"Teddy, I know you're in there."*

He's right. I'm in a bathroom the size of a broom closet, kissing the girl of my dreams, making sure she knows exactly how I feel about her.

There's no place I'd rather be.

EPILOGUE

One month later

Jane

These people are crazy. It's the first time I've been around them as a group since that night six weeks ago at the arena, and now I see what I've been missing. Teddy and his cousin are the wackiest of the bunch.

"I still don't see why you're doing this now," Teddy says, walking behind Liam like a lost puppy, holding onto a shirt he just removed from Liam's suitcase. For a country mega-super-star, he sure is whiny when he isn't happy. "Can't it wait until next month? What if you change your mind? What if you decide you're no longer compatible? What if you find out Dillon talks in her sleep and kicks really hard and sometimes wets the bed? What then?"

Dillon rips the shirt out of Teddy's hand and folds what he just unfolded. She looks so offended it's hard not to laugh.

"You haven't slept in the same bed as me since you were six years old," she says. "I only wet the bed once, but you act like I did it all the time."

"That's because you woke up and pushed me into it, and then pretended I wet the bed instead of you," Teddy protests.

"I woke up with dry pants, and I was so confused. Not to mention grossed out."

I'm grossed out just listening to them.

"Tell me about it," Liam said. "I had to live on an island with her, and she wet the bed all the time then."

"We didn't even have a bed, we had a beach! And we peed on palm trees, so none of that counts!"

"Gross, Dillon," Teddy says.

"Gross, Dillon," Liam says at the same time.

Now I am laughing, especially when Chad says from the computer screen:

"Gross Dillon. Hey, that's my shirt. I've been looking for it everywhere. Liam, unpack that right now. Teddy, bring it to the wedding. And if there's anything else that belongs to me, bring it, too." He's on Facetime from Springfield, using Teddy's laptop perched on the bedroom dresser so he can join the fun. It's a circus. They're all mad around here.

"You can have everything but the coffee maker," Teddy says.

"Can't you buy your own coffee maker, Teddy?" A blue-haired chick asks from the background. I think her name is Riley. I'll meet her next month and find out for sure. "You have like, a bazillion dollars."

"So do you, Riley. You can buy him a new one." Teddy says. She laughs and says she will, then kisses Chad's nose to soften his scowl. It works. I have no idea what anyone is talking about, but I'll find out later. "Besides," Teddy continues, "I like this one because it makes the best coffee."

"He's right, it does," Chad says.

"He's right, it does," Liam says too.

They're crazy, and they speak Parrot.

I wish blue hair would look good on me, but I can't pull it off. I tried it once and looked like Smurfette. Actually, she looked better than me.

"I'll let you have it if you stay here until the wedding," Teddy says to Liam.

"It's my coffee maker!" Chad protests.

Teddy just waves him off.

"First of all," Liam says, "you're lying. Second of all, I already rented an apartment in Brentwood. If I don't move in now, they'll give it to someone else." He places a hand on Teddy's shoulder. "You'll be okay without me, buddy. Use your blanket if you have nightmares."

Teddy flings Liam's arm away with a growl. "Piss off, jerk. It's just, this place is too big without roommates. I don't even like it that much. And I don't have a blanket...anymore." He mumbles that last word, but we all hear it.

"Then find another place. Or...get a roommate." I don't miss the way Liam's eyes flick to me.

"Don't look at me," I say. "I just rented my own place down the street, and it's a one-bedroom. A one-bedroom for *me* only," I point out when all three people in this room grow more intrigued. "We've only been dating a month," I mutter when no one looks away, and it seems I'm losing the argument.

But it's true. I'm not ready for that kind of commitment. Scratch that. I *am* ready, but I now know I deserve more than part-time or dangling promises. I'm very ready for a solid commitment with Teddy, but only if it comes with a ring.

A ring? Where did that thought come from?

Is it hot in here?

Is anyone else having trouble breathing?

"Leave Jane alone," Dillon says. "Sorry, Jane, you'll get used to this eventually. No one escapes a family gathering without a hard time, so consider yourself an official member now. Lucky you." At this, I laugh. There's no denying I feel more than a little lucky. These people are definitely strange, but they're also great. Something tells me this is what family is supposed to be.

"Yeah, lucky you," Liam says.

"Yeah, lucky you," Chad says.

"Yeah, lucky you," Teddy says. Except he winks.

And I smile.

Lucky me for sure.

———

Teddy

"Are you going to be okay?" Jane asks, sitting down next to me on the sofa. I set my guitar aside and pull her onto my lap, loving the way she fits so perfectly with me.

"I'll be fine. Things are changing around here. But they aren't all bad." I grip her waist and melt a little when she plays with my hair. "You're here, and you're a million times better than those guys." I bury my head in her neck and growl a little. "You smell good."

"Well, I did take a shower this morning, so at least I have that going for me."

"You have a lot more going for you than that." She squeals as I pull her across me and flip her on her back, then hover over her. It's a big sofa; I'll make it work.

Growing serious, she slides underneath me and looks up expectantly. If I've learned anything in life, it's that you should never disappoint a woman. It's illegal in forty-seven states.

She swallows, and I press my mouth lightly against hers. Her lashes lower, and it's all the permission I need. My teeth catch her bottom lip, and she grips the back of my shirt. My tongue touches hers. Her lips part, taking me in. She tastes like chocolate and spearmint, a combination I've quickly grown to love.

The thought no longer scares me and instead fills me with peace.

I love Jane. I've told her a hundred times, at least.

Her fingers dance across my back as mine slide upward and over, not too far, but also not far enough. The feel of her skin makes me crazy, but I know how to control myself. It's what we've agreed to for now. I shudder against my own weight and pull back a fraction to look at her.

"This okay?"

"Yes," she says, pulling me down for a longer kiss. This one grows more intense, and I feel myself cursing our little agreement. I can't think about it for too long. Just as I'm thinking about testing the waters a bit, she says the oddest thing.

"Something keeps buzzing in your pants."

I freeze and then realize what she means. With a sigh, I sit up and pull out my phone. My stupid, stupid phone. It's Dillon. She left thirty minutes ago. What does she want now?

Your outfit was waiting on my front porch when I got home. Can't wait to see you wearing it.

I grow numb with dread. This can't be good.

"Who was it?" Jane says, her legs still tangled with mine.

"Dillon." I roll my eyes and show her my phone. Within seconds, she's laughing.

"You think this is funny?"

"Hysterical." Her laughter grows.

"Oh yeah? Well, how would you like to be my date for the wedding? You won't be laughing when your date's walking around in a dress."

She pushes me back on the sofa and slides next to me, one leg draped across mine. "Of course, I'll be laughing. I'll be laughing my butt off. And I'd be honored to come. Besides, I wouldn't miss the sight of you in a dress. Think of all the money I'll make when I sell the photos to the tabloids."

She hovers over me, mere inches from my face. I run my hands across her back and settle them on the top of her hips. "I suppose worse things could happen."

"Worse things already have. It's only up from here."

I smile because she's right. Worse has already happened.

It *is* only up from here.

I pull her head down and kiss her again.

It's the only thing on my schedule for the rest of the day.

THE END

Please consider leaving a review of *The Last Shot* on Amazon and Goodreads.

OTHER BOOKS BY AMY MATAYO:

The Aftermath

The Waves

Lies We Tell Ourselves

Christmas at Gate 18

The Whys Have It

The Thirteenth Chance

The End of the World

A Painted Summer

In Tune With Love

Sway

Love Gone Wild

The Wedding Game

Amy Matayo

amymatayo.com

Amy Matayo is an award winning author of *thirteen books*. *Her book, The Whys Have It,* was a 2018 RITA Award finalist. She graduated with barely passing grades from John Brown University with a degree in Journalism. But don't feel sorry for her—she's super proud of that degree and all the ways she hasn't put it to good use.

She laughs often, cries easily, feels deeply, and loves hard. She lives in Arkansas with her husband and four kids and is working on her next novel.

Twitter: @amymatayo

Instagram: @amymatayo.author

Facebook: www.facebook.com/amymatayoauthor

The Aftermath

by

Amy Matayo

Riley Mae

"Order up, Buttercup."

"Riley Mae, I wish you would stop talking like that. The customers will think they're eating in a truck stop instead of a bakery. If you want to make franchising this place a thing, you need to act more like a professional and less like someone circling want ads in the back of the newspaper." My grandmother, God rest her soul, is the queen of lectures. She's also not dead. A good thing considering she is my only family, friend, and general person I can depend on for practically anything. Including regular lectures. The best news? I can give them back. I learned from the best.

"Two things about that," I say, slipping a potholder off my hand. "One, have you ever eaten in a truck stop before? Best food around, so don't knock it before you try it. Two, they don't even make newspapers anymore. Or if they do, no one reads them." This might not be true, but I don't have time for technicalities. "And there's nothing wrong with circling want ads. Lest you forget, I spent my entire senior year of high school doing exactly that."

"It's hard to get hired when you tell every manager in town that minimum wage is the unacceptable equivalent of child labor."

"That might have been a bit dramatic..."

"A bit? People saw you coming and locked up for the day. Mr. O'Dell at the grocery store still brings up that time Ron's Shake Shack closed before noon because you'd rattled the employees too badly."

"All I asked for was a tiny bit more money than he offered."

"You asked for thirty dollars an hour and called him a cheapskate when he said no. In front of the whole restaurant."

Why is my past always used against me to make a point?

"He deserved it. Do you know what high-schoolers make working fast food? It's shameful."

"They make what the rest of the country makes when they're sixteen and have no resume. Minimum wage."

"See? Child labor." Point for me. "Besides, I have my own business now, so I don't need anyone else to hire me. The American Dream in the flesh, who would have thought? *Order up.*"

"Living the American dream while throwing people off with that accent." Paul, our behind-the-counter-boy with, coincidentally, a *great* behind, grins at me as he swipes the plate off the counter and delivers it to table four. I watch him walk with a slightly guilty conscience because he's twenty and about nine years too young for me. Not that it should matter; I've even caught my grandmother checking him out a time or two. But it does matter, and I'm slightly bitter about what-might-have-been if God had created me a decade past my time. It's one of the first things I'll ask about when I get to heaven, assuming He lets me in.

"Stop checking out my backside, boss," Paul calls over his shoulder, and the whole restaurant laughs, mainly because they're all checking him out too. "Anyone else would sue you for sexual harassment. You're lucky I'm not just anyone, and that you're practically like my mom."

"You really know how to hurt a girl, don't you?" I call. "I'm only twenty-nine, in case you forgot."

He props an elbow on the counter and leans close to my face, making an effort to look smoldery and hot. It isn't that difficult. "So you're saying you would go out with me if I asked? You know I'm a sucker for the way you talk."

For a second I hold his stare and think about the possi-bility—he's so ridiculously good looking that *GQ* would wilt if he ever appeared on its cover. He's also attentive in the way college guys with one thing on their minds are attentive, except he's nice. So, what's the problem? Paul is my grand-mother's best friend's grandson, if you can keep up with that, and I've known him since infancy. I might have even helped change his diaper a time or two. I would find him hotter if that gross memory didn't plague me.

So, it's with a small sigh of longing that I pick up a clean towel and smash it in his face. Paul backs up and laughs, and I thank God once again that he agreed to work for me. Still, I have to correct something he said.

"For your information, I barely have an accent anymore. And second, no, I wouldn't go out with you. Besides, have you already forgotten about Amanda? Any minute now she'll walk in, and then you'll know why I've been talking about her so much."

Paul picks up the towel and tosses it on the counter, then reaches for another plate ready for table six. "If she's so pretty, maybe you should go out with her."

I shrug. "She's not my type. I go more for the young, male, college-age crowd. Especially the ones with dark hair and way too much confidence."

Paul laughs, his nearly black hair shaking with the motion, and darn it if I'm not once-again cursing the heavens at our unfortunate age difference. Nine years isn't that unheard of, is it? Celebrities do it. Lord knows presidents do it. I sigh. Loneliness is seriously messing with my mind. If the heavens could do something like, you know, send me a sign that I won't be alone forever, that would be great.

Instead, He sends me a customer waving a finger in the air like he needs help. I snatch an order pad off the counter and wander over to his table.

"Are you finally ready for your cupcake, James?" I ask. He's been here nearly an hour and has only had coffee which is not unusual for him. James is the kind who has to slowly justify his sweet tooth, though he always decides that it's permissible to have one.

"Sure am, Miss Riley. I can't wait to see what you have for me today."

I smile. "I had one in mind the moment you walked in the door wearing that red flannel shirt. Don't you know it's still hot outside, James? And today it's especially muggy. You need to retire that shirt so you don't die of a heat stroke. Hang on a second, and I'll get the one I picked out for you. Want more coffee too?"

"Of course. It'd be a sin to have dessert without coffee."

"Basically like breaking the eleventh commandment. There aren't enough Hail Marys in the world to redeem you from that."

James looks up at me and laughs, and I walk away to get his cupcake.

I do a thing here. It's something the customers have grown to expect. It's like my own little novelty, though, for the life of me I can't remember how it started. A couple years ago, I think? Maybe Paul's first day of work when he showed up ten minutes late, and I made a production in front of everyone, quickly scratching a clock out of a nearby bag of black icing on a white cupcake and handing it to him. *This says nine o'clock. Maybe now you'll show up on time tomorrow.* The customers laughed, and they've been requesting their own cupcakes since.

Make one for me, Miss Riley.

Make me one, Riley Mae.

It's a mantra of sorts, so I do.

I make cupcakes designed around people's personalities: good moods, bad moods, loud clothing, crass jokers. None of that matters to anyone, because when I hand them a cupcake that represents whatever I sense in them that day, they laugh. It's hard to stay down when your dessert becomes your shrink. Cupcakes make everyone happy, even ones decorated with butcher knives, blood, and tears. Just ask James. He came in frazzled and sweaty—partly due to that dang shirt. This will get him in a better mood.

I set a naked, showering, and soaped up Santa in front of him and wait for his reaction.

He blinks at it and narrows his eyes. "Christmas, Miss Riley? In September?

"You look like Santa in that shirt. Lumberjack Santa building his toys."

"Why's he taking a shower?"

"Because he's sweaty and stinky, that's why."

"Are you saying I smell bad?"

"Never." James has gray hair and a short gray beard. He would, in fact, look exactly like Santa if he grew it longer and wore a red sweater. I drop my voice to a whisper. "But if you must know, I have a little crush on the jolly guy. Don't tell anyone."

I wink, and he blushes, doing his best to hide a smile. See? Cupcakes change moods for the better. James is still sweating, but I suspect now it's for an entirely different reason.

Paul walks by with another plate and sets one down at a table by the front window, so I raise my voice to an unnatural volume.

"Especially don't tell Paul. I wouldn't want him thinking he has any competition."

Paul glances up at me and raises an eyebrow. "Don't tell Paul what?"

I shrug. "About my crush on James—I mean, Santa Claus. Oops, I guess the secret's out." I blow James a kiss and walk away to the sound of both men laughing.

"She's a mess," I hear Paul say, and I smile when James agrees with him. It's what I love about owning a bakery, maybe even more than the baking itself. The camaraderie.

The friendly banter and lightening of spirits. The sense of family ushered in with familiar faces that show up day in and day out. I'm comfortable here; more than comfortable. I belong. I have a home. It's been a long time coming for a girl who spent years hoping and praying just to feel included. Loss and abandonment will do that to a girl, even when she has a grandmother who cared enough to stick around through the hard parts. She's been there for me in ways no one else has, but it's sometimes easier to focus on the ways we're slighted.

I'm almost to the kitchen when out of nowhere, lightning strikes loud and unexpected. Startled, I clutch my chest and turn around. What in the world? An elderly customer dropped a fork, everyone else is momentarily frozen and staring out the window. The air is still, but nothing looks particularly out of the ordinary. I rush to retrieve another fork. That little bit of activity snaps everyone out of their trance, and the shop is buzzing with noise again.

"Here you go," I say, placing the fork next to her half-eaten cupcake, a strawberry one frosted white and laced with pearls. I look out the window and swallow, breathing slowly to calm my heartbeat. Old memories are impossible to shake, particularly ones that change your life. "Is it supposed to storm?"

"The news called for a thirty percent chance of rain today..." the woman mutters, looking out the window. "Well, would you look at that. Looks like more than thirty."

The sky that was bright and sunny only seconds ago has suddenly turned an odd shade of grayish-green. The air has taken on an almost medicinal hue, like sulfur has settled inside the molecules and decided to hang on for a ride. It's one o'clock in the afternoon but it looks dark enough to be near sunset. I stare another moment, then shrug and return to the counter. Customers are still waiting, and my staring out the window won't get anyone fed. I reach for a bowl of sugar packets for table seven just as a low rumble makes its way across the roof. An overhead light begins to sway back and forth.

"Ow!" my grandmother says.

"Be careful," I call over my shoulder, then set the platter down in front of a family of four. A mom, a dad, and two little girls wearing French braids, one child older than the other. It's the best part about Saturday afternoons; the way families come out to eat, children filling up the tiny bakery with laughter and mischief. Two crayons are on the floor, along with a half-eaten waffle. How that fell is anyone's guess.

Glancing up, I see that it's bright and sunny again. This weather is weird. Paul is still standing by the window, engaged in what seems like a serious conversation with a first-timer. The storm must have been nothing more than a passing cloud, thank goodness. Bad weather tends to chase away customers.

I refill another coffee and walk back to the kitchen to check on my grandmother. She's leaning against the sink with a wet cloth pressed to her wrist.

"You okay? What happened?"

"Oh, the light flickered back here, and I burned myself trying to get the cinnamon rolls out of the oven."

I frown at the red skin peeking out from under the towel. "That lightning strike was loud. I'm glad the lights didn't stay off." I wave a finger in the air, and she relinquishes her wrist. This isn't the first time my grandmother has hurt herself at work; she knows the drill. When I pull the cloth off, it's worse than I imagined. "Did you hold your wrist to the coils just to see how much pain you could take? You really burned it."

"I didn't do it on purpose. It took a minute for the light to come on, and I got confused for a second. Instead of jerking my arm back, I went up and accidentally pressed it against the heat."

The image rolls my stomach. "Stay here. I've got a first aid kit in the office, and I'll doctor it right up." I flip on the light in the small make-shift office and rummage through the metal desk drawers for bandages and ointment. I bought the desk at a re-sale shop two years ago and never oiled the hinges like I intended to. Consequently, the drawers squeak loudly every time they open and close. Imagine chewing tin foil during a particularly grueling toothache. That's what it sounds like.

"Are you ever going to oil that desk?" my grandmother calls. "It makes my chest hurt every time I hear it." It's the same conversation every single time, and she already knows the answer. Yes. No. Probably. Maybe.

"Yes, when I remember to buy WD-40, which we both know I'll never do. Keep up with my personality, grandma."

She laughs, and I'm relieved. At least the pain hasn't cut her sense of humor. I lean in close and pull back the cloth to carefully examine her wrist. It's disgusting. I used to think about becoming a nurse, but it's a good thing I didn't. Burns and splinters give me full-body chills, and right now is no exception. At least three layers of skin are burned though, maybe even four. I squeeze antibiotic ointment onto a bandage and smear it around with my finger, then secure it to her wrist, making sure the burn is completely covered. Burns are more common than you might think around here; the last thing anyone needs is an infection.

"Maybe you could get Paul to do it. You know, if you promise to go out with him or something. If nothing else, it would give him a reason to buy oil."

I raise an eyebrow because surely she didn't mean...

She did. Her wicked grin practically screams it. "Gross, grandma. I don't need Paul to take me out *or something*, and I definitely don't need him to oil my...desk. So, get your mind out of the gutter."

I twist the cap back on the tube of medicine a little too roughly. "Do I have to remind you he's a child? And my employee?"

"He might be younger than you, but he's hardly a kid. He'd go out with you in a heartbeat if you'd show him some interest."

"He's Julia's grandson! She would kill me, or is that part of your master plan?"

At this, she laughs again, finding way too much delight in my impending demise. Sometimes I wonder what life is like for ordinary people, ones whose grandmothers aren't so invested in their love lives. Shouldn't she have taken up knitting by now? Joined a bridge-playing group? Maybe you don't do that sort of thing when you've never mentally matured past age seventeen. More likely, you don't do that sort of thing when you're left with the task of raising a granddaughter as your own child. She didn't ask for that task, but she stepped up all the same.

She pokes me on the arm. "Oh, lighten up. I guess it is a little weird when you put it that way. Fine, you don't have to date Paul. But could you at least date someone before I die and never get to see you happy?"

There are so many things I could say to this, but I swallow them all and simply say, "I am happy. I don't need a man for that."

"I wish someone had told me that when I was younger. Would have saved me a lot of trouble." She means it as a joke, but I hear the deep regret buried in her words. Her good hand reaches out to stroke my hair in a rare display of seriousness. "Pink. I'm still not used to it, but I have to admit the color looks good on you."

I smile at the unexpected compliment. "It's temporary

and will probably fade fast, but thank you. I'm glad I finally did it. Took me a while to get brave enough." I've studied every shade of unnaturally-colored hair for months now, desperate to branch out and try something different. Life can get monotonous in a small town for a girl who's married to her job. This place doesn't offer much in the way of excitement or social life, not now or in the two decades since I showed up. It came down to skateboarding in Nathanael Greene Park or dyeing my hair a weird color.

It's sad when pink hair offers you the thrill you've been looking for.

My grandmother sighs. "You have more courage in your little fingers than most people I know. Have since you were seven..." Thankfully, her voice trails off. Some things aren't necessary to revisit, not out loud or inside the mind. "I just want to know that you're taken care of when I'm gone. It's all I've ever wanted."

I smile because I know. "You're not going anywhere, and personally I think I'm doing okay taking care of myself. I have this bakery after so many years of just hoping for it. I have you working here with me and customers who seem to like it. Other than opening up a second location and franchising it one day—fingers crossed—what more could I want?"

She shrugs. "Love?"

"I have you. It's all the love I need." My grandmother raised me to be strong and independent like her. It wasn't like she had a choice in the matter.

"Hush up, child. I'm not enough, and you know it." She pushes off the counter and waves me away, rubbing her wrist. It hurts, and that might bother me more than anything. I hate seeing her in pain, but it's becoming more common as she ages. One can act like they're seventeen all they want, but the body refuses to cooperate when it comes to aging.

"You *are* enough. You and Paul both. Who knows, maybe in ten years he won't be too young anymore. If nothing else, maybe he would agree to be my baby daddy. I'll be nearly forty and desperate at that point." I wink, and my grandmother shakes her head in exasperation.

"You won't need a baby daddy."

"You never know. I could be so busy running my twenty stores across the country, that

having a baby daddy is the only way I'll have time for kids. Someone should stay behind and help raise them, so why not Paul? Life is unpredictable that way. Plus, I could definitely do worse."

I could do *much* worse.

She laughs and walks out of the kitchen while I head back into the office to put away the medical kit. It's a mess back here, papers on the sofa and floor, the trash can overflowing with litter, and someone needs to clean it. That someone would be me, but whatever. I shove the medical kit in the top drawer and close it with my thigh. I'm leaving the room, picking at a snag on my thumbnail when it happens.

Lightning. Another strike, loud and violent. So violent the building shakes and the stack of papers on the desk float to the ground and scatter in a long wave of white. Wide-eyed and confused, I bend on shaky legs to retrieve them when something shatters in the other room. Loud and deafening, like a window breaking or plates tipping over. The building shakes again as the deafening roar of a freight train barrels through the bakery. I cover my ears to block out the noise, but it doesn't mute everything.

People scream.

Children cry.

Furniture splinters.

What on earth is happening?

In a panic, I crawl through the swinging doors and suck in

a breath, the wind too strong, the noise too loud, every part of me numb at what I see.

Broken glass. Swirling papers. Toppled furniture. Shattered dishes. Fathers are holding to the ankles of flailing, crying, children. Mothers are huddled in heaps underneath tables, trying to protect those around them, trying to get away from the roaring wind and flying debris. Upturned tables that were occupied only a few minutes ago. The picture window is gone. I see what looks like my grandmother's shoe. I don't see Paul at all.

Complete and utter chaos is all around me.

This is what shock feels like.

I'm frozen in place, blank for what to do. And then something brushes against my arm and snaps me into action. Paper. A person. A tape dispenser. I'm suddenly aware of everything around me. With pure animal instinct, I scream. I holler out a long stream of instructions to everyone and no one, a litany of demands with no room for argument. Trust me. I know what I'm doing.

"Hurry up! Everyone get in the kitchen! Crawl! Run! Straight through these doors! Keep your heads down!" People crawl past me while I count heads. One, two, seven, nine, where is my grandmother? Where is Paul?

It isn't until the room empties of people that I see my grandmother. She's flat on the ground on the other side of the counter, moaning under a barstool that tipped and trapped her beneath it. But that isn't the worst of it. A large piece of glass juts from her side from the broken picture window, and blood has already fanned in a sunburst on her white button-up shirt.

That's the worst of it.

"Grandma!" I rush to her side, colliding with a table leg on the way. The bruise feels immediate. Hair blankets my face in a blinding sheet, the wind whipping it into my eyes and mouth. Desperate to see, I hold my hair back in a fist and slide next to my grandmother, patting at her body, quickly trying to assess the damage while yelling in her face. "How bad are you hurt? How bad?" Something wet slides down my face. I grab the barstool, trying not to be carried away.

Tears. I'm crying.

"I'm okay," she yells back. "I just got in the way of the window. What is going on?"

That's when they sound. Tornado sirens are blasting the downtown area in an ill-timed warning... two minutes too late. My grandmother blinks up at me, her eyes wide with fright--the details of her face blur through my tears.

"A tornado?"

Water drips from my eyes and nose, but I nod. "I guess so. I'll get help."

"No!" she yells, gripping my arms. "Don't leave me." It isn't hard to see where her mind has gone. If I let it, mine will head that direction too. Something I might have allowed if times weren't desperate, and if I didn't have people in the back room depending on me.

"Where's Paul?" I yell when she won't let go.

"I don't know. He was standing by the window when it started." My stomach drops to the floor at her words, and I scan the room. Nothing.

I shake my head to clear it, determination taking over. One thing at a time. "I'll call 911. Don't worry. I'll get someone here. If I have to, I'll drive you to the hospital myself."

Crawling on my stomach, I make my way behind the counter and reach for the phone. My grandmother insisted on installing a corded phone when we opened. At the time, I considered the request silly and outdated—doesn't everyone use a cell phone nowadays? Thank God she didn't listen to me. This one has stayed locked into the wall and hasn't blown anywhere.

I dial 911 and press the phone to my ear, thankful the line still works while straining to hear through the deafening noise. Finally, I hear the faint sound of words and start yelling.

"I need help. I'm downtown, and my grandmother is wounded." I give the operator my address and answer a slew of what seem to be pointless questions. *Where is the wound? Are you applying pressure? Are you aware there's a tornado in the area and the wait may be several minutes?*

Despite the alarms, the verbal confirmation of a tornado is sobering.

How many minutes?

I try to offer my grandmother a reassuring smile, one I don't feel at all. Blood scares me, but chaos scares me more. There's nothing like panic to bring the memories back, memories that aren't welcome to either one of us. I shunned them years ago, never intending to acknowledge them again. Yet here I am, staring head-on at catastrophe with no opportunity to look away. Blood snakes a trail down my knuckles, and my pulse trips inside my throat.

With assurances they will be here soon, I hang up, grab a clean towel from under the sink and crawl back to my grandmother's side to wait. "The ambulance is on the way, but they're backed up. Said they would be here in ten minutes or so."

She nods, silent and wide-eyed. What if we don't have ten minutes? Seconds are precious when life is on the line. I should know, and I have a history of seeing time run out. What makes me think today will be different?

I shove my dark thoughts aside and smile down at my grandmother, unsure what to do with the towel in my hand. The glass looks so deep and moving it seems like too much of a risk. She's already lost a lot of blood. So, I smooth back her hair the way she once did to calm me as a child, resting the towel just under the cut to catch the trail of blood falling under her ribs. Smiling works to ease worry, at least that's what I'm counting on. Still, the only thing I can think is: *what if she falls asleep? What if we don't have ten minutes?*

Dear God, please give us ten minutes.

It's a mental prayer that plays on repeat while the wind howls all around us.

Minutes pass. An ambulance doesn't come.

Chad

I think I found a solution to the Miller's insurance claim that they can live with. It won't garner them as much money as they'd hoped, but it won't leave them penniless either. Sometimes in life, we have to take the hard knocks with the rewards and be thankful even when things don't work out according to plan, and this is one of those times. They planned to settle for a half-million dollars. Their reality is one hundred thousand, take it or leave it. Let me be clear: both scenarios were astronomical, but this one won't involve my head on the proverbial company platter, or my body buried in the local unemployment line.

I crunch a few more numbers and enter them in my laptop, then file the claim. They'll be given a check for one-hundred-seventeen-thousand dollars and twelve cents, to be exact. I know for a fact we're being generous. Flood insurance isn't common in Tennessee, but the Millers were one of the fortunate few who've paid for it. Claims filed for busted pipes at an old bed and breakfast are almost unheard of because they never pay out. Had their home not been listed with the historical society two years ago, this claim wouldn't be paid either.

The money covers damages and nothing else. Mrs. Miller will have to give up her dream of new furniture and double-paned windows for now. She's lucky she doesn't have to give up her house.

"What's up, Buttercup?" My brother Liam walks in the kitchen and reaches for a bowl, then takes out a box of Rice Krispies and fills it nearly to overflowing. A few pieces ping as they fall to the counter. I smile at the nickname and click submit, then close my laptop.

"Did we just step back two decades? I haven't heard that nickname in forever." I squint through the bay kitchen window and rub my eyes. It takes me a while to wake up, but it's worse on Saturday mornings, whether I'm working or not. I drain my coffee and stand up for more, happy to see a freshly brewed pot.

"I know, right? It flew out of my mouth like Mom was the one here saying it. I'm more disturbed about it than you are." He eyes the table. "You're working already?"

"It's almost noon, and I had a deadline. I would have had a very irate client if I didn't file their claim this morning. I can't handle another phone call from her, even though she won't be happy about this claim when I drop the news."

"You didn't make her rich?"

I blow out some air and spoon two heaps of sugar into my mug. "It's always the dream, and always the disappointment. I intend to down three more cups of this before composing an email to her. Ten minutes after I hit send, I should have a half-dozen messages telling me what a rotten insurance man I am."

"Cool. Is this what I have to look forward to when I join the firm? A bunch of clients who hate me?" My brother passed the bar last week and starts a new job at McCain, O'Connell, and Stephenson on Monday. They're the biggest law firm in Nashville, which probably also means they'll give him the biggest headache. I love my brother, but I'm secretly looking forward to witnessing him struggle. I immediately feel chagrined, considering he spent five days on a deserted island a few months back with no promise of being rescued. I suppose that was struggle enough.

I take a sip of coffee and swallow the taste of guilt. "If you're as lucky as me, it is."

Liam holds up his mug in a toast. "Awesome."

"Is there more? Please tell me there's more." Teddy, our roommate and the owner of this apartment, shuffles into the kitchen and slides onto a barstool looking more disheveled than I've seen him in a long time. I suppose I'm one to talk.

My hair is two inches longer than normal, and I haven't shaved in three days. But where my reasons are plain laziness, Teddy has a good excuse.

He's been traveling for over a month and got in late last night. After a three-day reprieve—the longest break he gets in a five-month span—he'll head back out to begin the overseas leg of the tour. The life of a musician is glamorous and enviable, sure. But it also leaves you exhausted as hell and missing your friends. We miss him too. This three-man apartment isn't quite the same with two, because when Teddy's away, Liam and I argue more. It's the downside of being brothers.

"There's more unless Liam drank it all."

"I didn't, jerk." He pours a cup for Teddy and slides it across the bar. "Are you hungover?" Teddy's head rests on his arms, his face buried in the counter.

"No, I'm not hungover. I'm exhausted. Where am I? What city do we live in? Is it Christmas yet?"

Liam grins at me, shaking his head. "It's September, idiot. Drink that and pretty soon you'll remember. I made it strong." Yet another downside of living out of a suitcase; life is a constant adventure, but you never know exactly where you are. I might feel sorry for Teddy if he didn't have the best life of anyone I know. Money, fame, talent, travel, the adoration of women everywhere. He's on the cover of a different tabloid every week, and last month he was listed as number twenty-three in *People's Sexiest Man Alive* issue. Twenty-freaking-three. The guy isn't hurting for anything.

He raises up on one arm and drains his coffee in a long pull, and I wince. That had to burn. Okay, maybe he's hurting for that. His cup clatters when he sets it on the counter and drops his head onto his arm once again. When he speaks, it's a muffled, familiar whine.

"My head's about to explode, and I think I've lost hearing in my left ear."

"You say that every time you come home, but by the next day it's always better," Liam points out. It's true, he does and it is.

Teddy's head comes up. "I know that, dipshit. But right now, I can't hear anything on this side and I'm worried I never will again." He points to his ear while I roll my eyes behind him and make faces he can't see. I'm aware this gives me the maturity level of a child; I'm also aware Teddy is fun to mock because sometimes he complains so freaking much. Liam leans against the counter, trying not to laugh.

"If you think I don't know what you're doing back there, you're wrong," he says to me. "I can see your reflection through the glass cabinet door. Cut your hair, by the way. It's too long." Teddy whips a dishtowel off the bar and hauls it backward like a man who's done it before. I don't manage to duck fast enough, so the damp towel lands on my face. It slides downward, leaving the scent of old onion and wet paper in my hair. I grimace and use it to wipe up a coffee ring. My hair is not too long, and there's nothing wrong with it or the twelve pounds I've taken off since last month. Sometimes when your life veers a different direction than you hoped for, you veer right along with it. Reinvention is the close cousin of heartbreak.

"You'll hear fine tomorrow," Liam says. "Today, though, you should stay in bed and sleep. I'll call for pizza tonight and stay in with you."

Teddy frowns and twists back around to face Liam. "You're offering to stay in with me instead of going out with Dillon? What gives?" Dillon is Liam's fiancée, and I'd like to hear the answer to this question as well. The two have been inseparable since their engagement, something that took me some time to get used to. Before my brother began dating

Dillon, I dreamed of her. Hoped and prayed to date her myself. Now that he has her, I'll kill him if he lets her go. I didn't suffer the loss of an imaginary future with her for nothing.

He looks between us like a frat boy caught with two women. "Nothing gives." So much guilt camped inside those two words.

Teddy and I stare at him, waiting.

He runs both hands down his face. "Fine. I don't want to taste wedding cakes again, but that's all she can talk about. *Should we go with the strawberry cream or the raspberry coconut or the vanilla caramel?*" he mimics in a high-pitched voice. "What even is raspberry coconut? Chocolate. It's the only choice. No one wants strawberry cream."

I shudder. Teddy shudders. "If you pick strawberry cream, I'm not coming to the reception," he says.

"Me either."

I see Liam's jaw clench from here. "You're my best men. You have to come and give toasts."

"Then pick chocolate, or you'll hate what I have to say."

"Ditto."

"Do either of you ever have your own separate thoughts?" Liam asks us both.

"Nope," we both say in unison.

And it's mostly true, especially about food. We're a chocolate group through and through. Don't believe me? Check out our pantry. Oreos are stacked five packages deep, and the Reese's peanut butter cups have their own special corner complete with a *Candy Only* label.

"Now that the cake's settled, yes pizza," Teddy says. "Chad, you in or out?"

I run a finger around the coffee cup rim. "Can I let you know later?"

"Sure, but you need to be here." Liam says, settling the

matter. Then he hones in on Teddy again. "Dude, did you see this cover?" He picks up a *US Weekly* and flips it around to show us the front. "It says here you're dating her. But this one..." he turns over a *Star*, "claims you're dating *her*." One girl is an A-list actress, the other a well-known fashion model. Both of whom any red-blooded American and non-American man would kill to be photographed with. "What I want to know is..." Liam continues, "Which one is true?"

Teddy rolls his eyes. "They're both true. I'm dating them at the same time, and I've got three more chicks waiting in the wings, *and* the new Marvel hero is giving me serious consideration. It's exhausting to be me, what with all the making out I must do on a round-the-clock schedule. I barely have time for touring, much less writing new songs. The real question is, why do you buy that crap?"

"To annoy you, of course." Liam grins and tosses the magazines down. "I'm tired just thinking about it. One girl is more than enough, though I'm fully invested in the Marvel chick. Let me know how that one works out for you."

"You'll be the first to know."

Liam's phone rings and breaks up this three-ring circus, and he picks it up. "Good morning, baby. You having a good day so—? Wait. What? No, I hadn't heard..." I stuff down a residual pang of jealousy as he walks down the hall and closes his bedroom door.

"I see you're still struggling," Teddy says, drilling a tiny hole in my conscience.

"Only a little," I admit. I hate being called on my crap, but it's also nice to be known without judgment.

"Give it time, and it will go away." He's right, but I don't respond. There's no need. We both know I can't wait for the day I wake up no longer pining for my brother's fiancée. After a couple of seconds, Teddy pats the countertop and stands up. "Alright, I'm heading back to bed. I'll see you tonight, okay?"

I nod, distracted. "Okay."

He takes a few steps, then doubles back for the magazines and swipes them off the counter. "I guess I should catch up on my fake love life," he says with a smile.

I laugh, though it fades into melancholy as Liam wanders back in with a look on his face. I've seen that look before, but it's been a while. It's like an ache before the flu sets in. Worried, but not feeling quite entitled to the emotion.

"Did you hear the news?"

"About Teddy's love life? A few dozen times too many, I'm afraid." I laugh and so does Teddy, but Liam's eyebrows furrow.

"No, about Springfield, Missouri. They had a massive tornado a couple hours ago. They're speculating over a hundred people are dead, maybe more. Supposedly it's worse than Joplin."

My stomach sinks into my shoes. Joplin was catastrophic. All these years later, and I'm not sure that town ever fully recovered. Yet this one is worse? That's hard to imagine, but I do, and what my mind conjures up leaves me unsettled, worried, and sick. It's another example of how life can change on a dime even when you'd rather feel penniless.

A hundred people dead. What must that town look like?

"Man, Missouri is not a place I'd want to live," Teddy quips, rolling the magazines in a tube inside his fists.

"Nor me, though sometimes Tennessee can be just as bad," Liam says. He's right because he knows firsthand. We both know.

"What are we going to do?" I ask, more to myself than anyone else.

Teddy sighs, long and slow. "Well, I'm going to take a nap."

Liam shrugs. "And I've got to call Dillon back. Pizza tonight, don't forget."

I scratch my eyebrow, wishing I had it in me to be so flippant and unconcerned. *"You're not an athlete like your brother, and you don't have his looks. And with that bleeding heart of yours, you're gonna have to prove yourself another way. Like, be a hero or become a millionaire. And snagging a hot wife wouldn't hurt."* My dad's oft-spoken words rush back like they always do, not at all concerned that I resent them like a leech already half-filled with my blood. I've spent my life proving myself. I've chased storms, chased heroics, chased women, chased anything that takes those words away. In all that time, I have managed to make a few lives better, but the girl is still elusive. Maybe someday, though it's looking less and less likely.

I'll settle for helping others out.

I watch as they both leave the room, then pick up my coffee and turn toward the window, staring at the iron railing that encircles the balcony. A robin is perched on one corner, the occasional burst of music bursting from his bill. Another bird lands at the other end and hops a bit closer. They're together, those birds, in the way nature pairs living creatures off and forms a family. I've never been jealous of birds before, but here we are.

Maybe it's the sound of Liam's voice drifting down the hallway as he talks in low tones to Dillon once again. Maybe it's the way Teddy is adored by so many...the number of women so vast the tabloids can't agree on who he should date next.

Either way, everyone has a person. Everyone has a place to belong.

"You're gonna have to prove yourself..."

I watch the birds and slowly sip my coffee.

Made in the USA
Coppell, TX
01 July 2023

18677717R00142